MY HARD BARGAIN

MY

HARD BARGAIN

Stories

WALTER KIRN

Alfred A. Knopf   New York   1990

THIS IS A BORZOI BOOK
PUBLISHED BY ALFRED A. KNOPF, INC.

Copyright © 1987, 1988, 1989, 1990 by Walter Kirn
All rights reserved under International and
Pan-American Copyright Conventions. Published
in the United States by Alfred A. Knopf, Inc.,
New York, and simultaneously in Canada
by Random House of Canada Limited, Toronto.
Distributed by Random House, Inc., New York.

Some of the stories in this collection were
originally published in *Esquire, The Quarterly,
Shenandoah, Southwest Review,* and *Story.*

Library of Congress Cataloging-in-Publication Data
Kirn, Walter.
My hard bargain / by Walter Kirn. — 1st ed.
        p.   cm.
ISBN 0-394-58303-5
I. Title.
PS3561.I746M9   1990
813'.54—dc20   89-71662
                                        CIP

Manufactured in the United States of America
First Edition

For Penny, Andy, Walt, and Millie.

With thanks to Pat, Will, and Gordon.

Contents

MY HARD BARGAIN

PLANETARIUM

ELDER JOHANNSEN became our bishop when Elder Rivers, our old bishop, left. For weeks and weeks, no one knew where Elder Rivers had gone, or why he'd gone. He'd simply disappeared. Soon, nasty rumors began to spread, and finally they got so bad that my father, the ward treasurer, had to stand up at a Testimony Sunday and calm down the congregation. He waved the building-fund bankbook in the air and told us there was nothing missing. He handed the book to a deacon, who passed it along the pews. Because people trusted my father—a lawyer and a CPA—none of the brothers or sisters opened the book to check things for themselves. My father stood

3

there patiently until the book was back in his hands, then he offered a crisp little prayer and sat back down.

When Elder Rivers's first postcard arrived a week or two later, the men were free to elect a new bishop. It came addressed to the whole ward, but I was one of the only people who read the card before my father drove it to Salt Lake to help in Elder Rivers's excommunication. The card had a stamp from the Philippines and showed a flock of birds with bright pink feathers landing on a hut. The message was cheerful. Elder Rivers had found a new wife, the daughter of someone he had known in World War II, and was planning on starting a big Catholic family. He promised to send along more cards whenever he had news.

Those cards went straight to Salt Lake, though. Only the highest Mormons ever saw them.

Not everyone at church agreed that Elder Johannsen was the right choice for bishop. I heard some talk in the halls about his mustache, questioning if it was necessary. But when it came time for the congregation to second his appointment, everybody's hand went up at once. Some people even stood, especially some women. Also the basketball players he coached on the church team.

I was one of those players. I knew Elder Johannsen well. He'd taught me how to set and shoot, he'd taught me how to foul and not get caught.

Like most big men, Elder Johannsen was slow on the break, though his bad knees gave him a good excuse. At Brigham Young University, when he'd been young and healthy, nobody on the court could touch Elder Johannsen, and he had the plaques and trophies to prove it. Even so, he boasted sometimes, but never for long and only after practice. He bragged to us when he was driving us home, when he was tired and couldn't help it. You knew he was tired when he rubbed his knees. Sometimes he took prescription pain pills and didn't drive so well.

4

We kept this to ourselves. We liked our coach.

While Elder Rivers had been our bishop, I'd never said a word about my problem. Once every couple of months, like every other Mormon, I went to my local bishopric to talk about my sins. The meetings were face-to-face, no screen between us like the Catholics had, and they usually started out with small talk: what we thought of certain trades in baseball, how I liked my summer job. If Bishop Rivers was rushed, though, he'd move right away to the list of questions that every Mormon bishop had to ask. The first question was always the same: "Have you committed murder?"

"No."

That was the easy one. The next few questions were not so easy. But when Bishop Rivers got past the crimes—the ones that you wouldn't be there if you'd done them—and down to the smaller personal matters, like had you drunk any Coke or beer, or had you looked at a girl with lust, then it got very uncomfortable. The fact was, Bishop Rivers knew you had done these things, you yourself knew you'd done them, and on top of that, you knew *he'd* done them. He would speed through the questions, keeping his head down, and you could tell that he wanted all noes by how he didn't leave you any time for yeses, which would have needed long explanations.

Bishop Johannsen did things differently, though. He raced through the felonies, not even breathing, but he let the smaller questions slowly float, like high, hanging jump shots.

"Now, Karl, have you masturbated?"

The clock on his shelf of trophies ticked and tocked. Outside the window, out in the world, a baby was being born every second. I noticed dust in the air.

"Yes," I said.

His next question was, "How often?"

That right there made me respect him: the way he was on the ball enough to follow up with, "How often?" Bishop Rivers

5

would have let it go—he would have pretended I'd done it just once. That it was possible to do it just once.

Bishop Johannsen asked again: "How many times, Karl?"

I told him. The number that came from my mouth amazed me. Not only was it a high number, it was exact.

Maybe I'd never confessed to my sins, but somehow I'd always been sure to count them.

"Well, cut it out," Bishop Johannsen said. "Just cut the whole thing out."

I looked him in the eye. "I will."

But that didn't work, and two months later I was back in there, giving another specific number. And that's when Bishop Johannsen and I really got down to business. That's when he laid his hands on my head, blessed me, and put me in his special team-wide program.

THE DAY MY MOTHER caught me masturbating I was standing in the living room, thinking that I was alone in the house. An ad for ladies' electric razors had just come on the radio. The announcer used the words *bikini lines*. He used them over and over. The next thing I knew my jeans were down and it was in my fist. I mashed it around for a minute, I jacked and I pulled, and just when I almost had it, had my orgasm, I looked to the side and saw my mother staring in through the picture window. She had on her gardening clothes and held a rake.

I zipped myself up, sat down on the couch, and waited for her to come inside, stand in front of me, and look down. I tested some different positions for my legs—kicked out straight and tucked in close, crossed and uncrossed—hoping to find the right one, the one that would make me look like a boy just sitting there on a couch. There had to be a right position, because there was a right everything.

My mother never came in, though. She stayed in her garden for hours, weeding.

A couple of days later, my father said at dinner: "I hear you have a private life now, Karl. Well, good luck with it."

My mother backed him up: "Good luck."

I had never wanted a private life. I had never asked for one. But that is what my parents gave me that night, and it didn't take long for me to realize that a private life is the world's worst punishment. My parents must have already known that.

My father bought a security chain and hooked it up inside my bedroom door, which I had always left open a crack to let in light from the hallway. He told me to keep the door shut from now on. He gave me sixty dollars from his wallet, three new twenties, and told me to spend them on things for my room. Buy whatever you want, he said—a record player, dirty books, posters of Farrah Fawcett, whatever. If you like something, go ahead and buy it, he said. Just don't think twice. This is *your* room now.

He backed out the door, shaking my hand. He turned away and I chained myself in.

I didn't have to buy new things. My room slowly changed on its own. After I finished my homework each night, I lay on my bed with my pants around my knees, tickling my cheek with my free hand, and watched the changes happen around me. My soft white gym socks snuck out of their drawer and ended up next to my bed in a stained, crusty pile. A dust web in the corner of the floor began to trap flies, which attracted a spider. My desk lamp came unplugged and stayed that way. My World Book Encyclopedia got out of alphabetical order.

Finally, I got so bored that I bought a phone with the twenties. I couldn't talk to my Mormon friends because their families had rules about phone use, so I called in orders for sausage pizzas and had them sent to hospitals and schools. I phoned up schools and hospitals and asked them if they'd ordered pizzas.

And always when I masturbated, I thought of two things: bikini lines and Sundays at church, when I passed out the sacrament trays with tainted fingers.

DURING OUR SECOND meeting, after he'd laid his hands on my head to give me his Melchizedek priesthood blessing, Bishop Johannsen went back to his desk and read me a list of practical tips for curing masturbation. The tips came out of a paperback book—I'd heard them all before. Keep your hands above your blankets, wear two pairs of underwear, never linger sitting on the toilet.

Bishop Johannsen closed the book and looked for a moment at the back cover. The title I read on the front was: *Nurse Rebecca's Words to Teens in Doubt*. Bishop Johannsen cocked his wrist and winged the book sidearm across the room, into the trash can.

This was a show-off move, I found out later. Gary Greene, who came in after me, told me that Bishop Johannsen made the exact same throw for him.

"Those techniques don't work," Bishop Johannsen said. "Chances are, you've already tried them."

I nodded. I'd thought of trying them.

Bishop Johannsen slid back in his chair. He opened his desk drawer against his stomach. His hand fished around in the drawer for a moment. He took out a yellow marking pen.

He pushed the marker across his desk at me.

"Two things I want you to do, Karl. I want you to buy a large black sheet of paper, poster-size, and every time you masturbate, I'd like you to use this special pen to make a little X on the paper. Okay?"

I shrugged. "Sure," I said. "You mean I shouldn't try to stop?"

"Try this idea of mine and you *will* stop," Bishop Johannsen told me. "I'm having all my players do it, the whole team. This pen has invisible ink, see—it only shows up with black light. I'm giving you boys a month to mark your posters, and then I'll collect them and post them in the locker room. I'll call a special team meeting then, screw in a big black bulb, and switch it on. We'll count our yellow *X*'s together. We'll get a chance to see what's what. No hiding."

"But if I do stop," I said, "then I won't have to make any marks, right?"

"You can't stop," Bishop Johannsen said firmly. "Don't even try. That's pure pride if you think you can do this alone. Even if you succeeded, you'd just go around with your head up. And then you'd fall even further, Karl."

He stood up out of his chair. I heard his knees pop. When I stood up with him and turned to leave, I looked in his open desk drawer and saw a whole carton of yellow markers.

PRESEASON BASKETBALL practice started that Tuesday night. We razored open the boxes of new shorts and jerseys and argued about which numbers we wanted. Conversions over the summer had given us three new players to replace the guys from last year who'd gone away on foreign missions. The new guys got their pick of the numbers, the opposite of how it was on school teams. We treated converts well in our ward. We wanted them to feel our love.

Going home, I rode in Bishop Johannsen's Buick along with Mark and Gary and one of the converts, Ricky, a Mexican. Because of where Ricky's house was—in a faraway part of Provo that he couldn't give clear directions to—the ride was a long one. Once we'd fastened our seat belts, Bishop Johannsen gave a short speech on what he thought our chances were that season—mixed, he said—but from then on, until I got out of the car, no one talked or looked at each other, though three of us were best friends.

Maybe because he'd taken his pain pills, Bishop Johannsen missed my turnoff. He cursed out loud when he saw what he'd done—I was just getting ready to tell him—then he drove in reverse for a quarter mile, scaring everyone.

I couldn't fall asleep that night. I thought about cleaning my room, but I never got around to it. In the morning, after breakfast, I spread out the black sheet of paper on my desk and chalked up three invisible X's. I wondered how many marks my teammates had, if my friends were as honest as I was.

WE PLAYED OUR FIRST two games away, knocking off other church teams that usually beat us badly. Ricky started at guard, in my old spot, and the two other converts also started. Those of us who'd been benched took it as a spiritual challenge. We clapped and cheered as loud as we could, trying to prove to the other teams' fans—Evangelical Lutherans and Seventh-Day Adventists—that Latter-day Saints were the best sports in town.

Even while I clapped and yelled, though, I was feeling sorry for myself, cut off from my friends and from Bishop Johannsen, whose coaching had turned too professional. All he wanted to do was win this year. Down in the locker room, under the chapel, he'd hung up a black-and-white photo of his old Brigham Young University team. He pointed to it at halftimes and told us about those players' records, their skills, and their enthusiasm. The converts loved this sort of thing. Myself, I had to work to keep my chin up.

I got there late the night of Bishop Johannsen's special meeting. I couldn't believe we were still going to have it. But Bishop Johannsen had called me that morning and had said in his calmest, kindest voice that one month was up and I should come at seven. I got there late because I rode my bike. He'd offered me a ride, but I'd said no.

The bulb in the church basement locker room hadn't been changed yet when Bishop Johannsen took my poster and taped it up next to the other ones. In the white light, the posters still looked blank and black. At a quarter to eight there were still people missing, including Ricky. In fact, we never saw him again. His parents changed their minds about our church and went back to being Catholic.

We sat on the bench in our street clothes while Bishop Johannsen screwed the black bulb in, standing on a chair. He did not have us pray while we waited, but some guys prayed anyway. Other guys quietly laughed and kidded each other.

Gary slid up beside me on the bench and whispered in my ear, "You better have more than twenty, Karl. I made a deal with Orrin and Phil to all go over twenty."

I looked at him. I hadn't heard about this.

Bishop Johannsen got down off the chair, stepping stiffly because of his knees. He looked at the posters, then turned around and said, "How many guys put their names on these? Anyone? If you did put your name on, show me where you put it and I'll be glad to tear it off."

Nobody moved or made a sound.

"Okay then," Bishop Johannsen said. "Good. Names aren't the point here. This isn't about embarrassment tonight. It's so that you can see yourselves the same way God sees you. With clear vision."

Somebody chuckled.

"Whoever just laughed has a lonely soul," Bishop Johannsen said. Then he turned off the white lights and turned on the black one.

First, I saw my bishop's hands. They glowed. Then as my eyes adjusted to the dark of the locker room, I saw our *X*'s emerging out of the wall like yellow stars. They floated in the purple dark. I'd thought that I would want to count them, but there were too many—they streamed out toward me, they shone in bands and columns. The room had a Mentholatum smell that made some players' eyes water. We sat there, breathing, watching, not talking. Our sins were yellow stars that ran together. I wanted to stay there all night, just looking.

ON

SET-ASIDE

Axel Munsen was sick in bed, recovering from a pesticide mishap—his wife and his father were doing all the work. His wife had a real job, off the property, selling microwave ovens in town at a liquidations warehouse. As a reward for her salesmanship, she had won a number of oval brass plaques that hung on the wall above her dresser, where Axel couldn't miss them. On mornings when he forgot to draw the blinds, the sunlight hit the plaques directly, causing a painful glare.

Axel's father did not work for plaques but to keep himself busy. He worked around the yard and in the outbuildings, getting up various projects for himself that were growing more ambitious every day. He didn't have any field work to do because the land was on Set-Aside this year, and would be for years to come. Though Axel should have felt blessed that such a government program existed—monthly checks for letting weeds take over— what he felt instead was confused. Now and again, before the accident, Axel had walked in the fields with his father, amazed at how tall and splendid these plants were that he had struggled so long to eradicate.

All of this was on Axel's mind as he sat up in bed that morning, sipping a chalky weight-gain mix and looking down through the window at his father sorting fence posts in the driveway. The radio on the bedside table was giving the opening prices in Chicago. Although it did not affect him anymore, Axel still liked to keep track of the market. Other shut-ins followed soap operas; Axel followed sorghum futures.

He watched his father sort the posts and thought about what was scheduled to happen later on in the day. A truck was going to come, with animals—his father's latest scheme. The Set-Aside program had taught Axel's father that you could indeed get something for nothing, and from this discovery he had deduced that for next-to-nothing you could get a lot.

The man was building a petting zoo.

He claimed it would draw in traffic from the highway and make them all rich.

But Axel wasn't impressed. His family had been rich before— several times, in fact. His wife had called it being "rich on paper," but Axel hadn't quite seen the distinction. Wasn't *all* money on paper? What Jenny had meant, he assumed, was that all those times they'd been rich in the past—when land was high and gas was low and there was a feeling the suburbs were spreading farther and farther out from the city—they hadn't really been rich at all because they hadn't been willing to sell yet. What they'd done instead was to borrow, modernizing the whole operation in order to push up their yields. And it worked. They had a record harvest. But so did everyone else that year because everyone else had modernized too, and then Axel's family was poor again. So their latest windfall, from Set-Aside, was money earned for doing nothing.

Axel finished his drink, feeling sleepy, and watched his father working in the sun. The only reason to work was if you liked it — this was what Axel had come to believe after all these weeks in bed. He'd realized some things about money, too: that it was all on paper and that it didn't exist.

A X E L ' S   C L O C K   R A D I O woke him at noon in time for the midday farm report. In just the last three hours, he learned, December corn had gone through the ceiling on news of a worsening drought. Axel did not know how to feel about this. You could root for the weather or root for the prices, you couldn't root for both.

He got up out of bed and dressed himself and walked down the hall to the bathroom, pleased by how strong and steady he felt. He wasn't going to push it by looking in the mirror, but the nausea was gone, the wobbly vision, and that was enough encouragement for now. He washed his hands and face, scrubbing hard to bring the blood up, then opened the jug of purified water his wife had set out on the sink for him and slid a paper cup from the dispenser. After taking a handful of pills — vitamins and minerals mostly — he dropped his trousers and got on the toilet and shut his eyes and waited, concentrating. At times like this, feeling his bowels move, he tended to think of himself as transparent, or as one of those science class see-through figurines. The faces on those anatomy models had a composed, eternal stare, and it was this expression that Axel imagined he would be left with once he had finally shitted and pissed and puked and rinsed himself clean.

His father called up the stairs, "You need any help up there?"

Axel looked behind him, satisfied, then flushed the toilet. Getting better, he had to believe, was a matter of sheer sustained expulsion, of voiding and replenishing.

"I'm fine," he said. "I think I'll be coming down."

"You want to try eating some lunch?" his father said.

"I'll know when I get down," said Axel. "I hope you're not smoking a cigarette, though. I don't want to smell that smell right now."

Axel leaned forward, got set, and stood up slowly from the toilet, feeling the weight flow into his legs like dense hydraulic fluid.

WHEN AXEL WALKED into the kitchen— the trip downstairs had been no big deal, he'd stopped to catch his breath just once and only for a moment—the smell that flew at him was not of tobacco but of burning cooking oil. He leaned against the doorframe and watched his father prepare his specialty: bite-sized deep-fried hamburger balls, crisp on the outside, raw in the center. Axel wished his old man would hurry up and pull the pan off the blaze, but he said nothing.

"There's salad," said Axel's father through the smoke. "Jenny tore up some lettuce. Nice and fresh. Unless you want some of this heart-attack food—"

Axel was making his way toward the table—there, he was sitting down. "I'll try the salad," he said.

His father nodded and switched off the stove. With a long spoon, he lifted the meatballs out of the grease and plopped them onto his plate. Axel looked on and tried to decide if his father was getting fat. The man had gained weight, it was clear, but the bulk started so high up—almost at his chest—that it was more like a wall than a paunch, an evenly advancing wall.

"There," said Axel's father, settling into his chair and sliding the bowl of salad toward his son. "We both have our food."

Axel picked up a fork, but the lettuce looked too cold to him, too icy—he thought he would let it warm up for a while. His illness had made him fastidious, picky, a thing he'd never thought he'd be.

"Now here's the deal," his father said, talking through a wad of chewed-up burger. "I'm getting the pens in shape, I've stocked the feed—I'll bet you can't guess what a red-tailed hawk eats."

"Just to be clear on this," Axel said, "who's going to actually care for these animals? Who's going to keep them clean and happy so people will want to touch them?"

"I am," said his father. "Me. —I thought we already went over this."

"You and Jenny went over it," said Axel. "You were afraid to go over it with me."

His father looked down at his plate, twirling a meatball in a pool of ketchup. "That's not true," he said.

"You were afraid I'd ask questions," Axel said. "For example: When all these cars drive up, who's going to be there to greet them? Somebody has to sell the tickets."

His father looked up. "That's easy. People can put their money in a can. I'll run it on the honor system."

Axel picked up his fork again and poked at a frozen lettuce leaf. "Fine," he said. "You can make it free, for all I care. Just don't ever ask me to feed those animals."

"But that's the whole trick," his father said, grinning. "We'll get the tourists to feed them *for* us. We'll sell them little cups of grain at fifty cents a pop!"

For a moment Axel almost grinned himself. He had to admire

his father sometimes. The man had practically no education and yet he was nobody's fool, except his own.

"I see your point, though," his father said, spearing another gory meatball. "I know there's going to be work to do. But once you lay eyes on these animals, Axel—that red-tailed hawk especially—"

"The hawk," said Axel. "I'm sure it eats mice. That's very interesting. We used to set traps for mice, but now we'll have to breed them or something."

His father put down his fork and said, "You're feeling all right today, aren't you? Well, I have a question, too: Why don't you put that salad in your mouth instead of just giving it funny looks? Then I could take you outside and show you what I've been up to. —This attitude of yours is for the birds."

Axel locked eyes with his father, then scraped back his chair, stood up, and turned his back. He filled a glass of water from the tap, drank the water, then drank some more.

"Jenny and I had a talk with your doctor," he heard his father say. "We think it's time you got outside."

Axel turned off the tap.

BEFORE HE'D ENROLLED in the Set-Aside program and made himself independent of the weather, Axel had not automatically thought of warm, sunny days as "nice." A day was nice if it brought you what you needed. Today, though, without any stake in rain, Axel was letting his senses decide, and they told him that it was a nice day indeed. The only reason he had on a sweater was that he wanted to sweat.

Axel sent his father on ahead—the man had a lot to do before the truck came—and stood on the porch for a while, reacquainting himself with the view. He saw that the lawn was scorched and overgrown, particularly around the elm stumps, but overall it looked okay. The circle of stones that set off the birdbath needed another coat of white paint, but that would only make the house look faded. When the place had first come down to Axel from his father—not in a formal transfer of deed, but in a reversal of who gave the orders (the man becoming hesitant and quiet, his ag-school graduate son growing firm)—Axel had tried for a couple of summers to raise the yard to a groomed, suburban standard, everything trimmed and bordered and square. But the effort was futile. To keep a lawn in shape you needed children, and Jenny's doctor had nixed that from the start. Things fell apart completely once the old man got in on the act, embellishing the yard with relics: broken-spoked wagon wheels, cow skulls nailed to trees, battered milk-can planters. For a while, the yard had resembled a settlers' cemetery. Now it resembled a field.

It was a field.

Axel stepped down off the porch and crossed the yard, measuring out his breaths like level teaspoons of medicine. He thought he could hear his father sinking fence posts behind the machinery shed. That was where the zoo would be, Axel's wife had told him—far from the house so the smells wouldn't carry and he could keep the bedroom windows open.

"Put your shirt on," Axel said when he found his father. "Look how red your shoulders are."

His father put down the posthole digger and picked up his flannel shirt off the ground, toweling off his neck with one of the filthy sleeves. "Turn around and look up," he said. "Would you stop your car for a sign like that?"

Axel looked where his father was pointing—up at the east-facing wall of the barn. The painted design was so tall that Axel had to step back a few feet to take it all in. A monstrous yellow "happy face" formed the blinding centerpiece, surrounded by partially filled-in sketches of what he could only assume were the animals. One sketch seemed to represent a deer, another one vaguely suggested a fox, and then there were several smaller forms that Axel could not make out at all—rabbits they might have been, or geese. And while the deer and the fox were obviously pictured in profile, with only one eye apiece, they both had curving, front-facing smiles.

Axel turned and faced the man. "I hate to tell you right out like this, but I don't want this trash on my barn," he said. "This isn't Disneyland, Dad—it's where we live."

His father looked down at the ground for a moment, then off to the side, then back at Axel. "It's the best I could do," he said. "I could have had a professional paint it, but I was advised against that by the man I'm buying these animals from. He told me that signs for this type business *ought to* look homemade."

"I don't care. It's trashy," Axel said. The edge in his voice surprised him a little—he turned back around and checked the sign just to make sure his anger was justified. It was. "You said you were buying a few wild animals, then you said you were going to charge to see them, and now it's full-blown tourist shit," he said. "Jenny doesn't care because she's never here, but I'm having serious—" Axel stopped to catch his breath.

"I've already sent the check," his father said. "Let's just see how things go. This is my future, Axel—it's something I can do."

When Axel tried to answer this plea, his breath was not yet caught. He wheezed and started to cough—a rubbery flutter from deep in his lungs where the pesticide had settled.

His father said, "Take that sweater off. Sit down. Sit on one of those boards over there."

Axel waved him off. "I mean it," he said. "This whole idea has gotten out of hand. Today, you mentioned a hawk. Before, it was just a deer and a bear cub. Now I see a fox up there. And what are all those little shapes, those blobs?"

"Ferrets," his father said softly. "They come with the total package. I can't pick and choose—it's a used zoo."

"And what's a zedonk?" Axel whispered, feeling his head start to spin. "Up on the sign it says, 'See the zedonk.'"

His father watched Axel kneel and sit down. "I was about to tell you," he said. "I'm getting a couple of crosses and freaks. According to this guy I'm dealing with, freaks are what people want to see most."

Axel sat down on the ground, not hearing, putting out one arm to brace himself. He rubbed his eyes, he blinked and squinted, somehow convinced that the streaks he was seeing were actually on the surface of his eyeballs. He'd seen the same patterns the day of the accident, after he'd noticed the leaking valve and was standing there, trying to think, being stupid, watching the bubbles fizz through the seal and sniffing what smelled like chocolate hair spray. . . .

Everything went black as Axel felt the sweater being pulled off over his head. He held up his arms the way hostages do.

He heard his father say, "There we go."

Then his father said, "Look at you: you're soaked."

Axel fingered his T-shirt, pulled it away from his chest. His sweat had not felt the same since that day. It felt more like paste than water.

"Let's get you out of the sun," his father said. He hooked Axel's armpit and helped him up and walked him to a grassy spot under the eave of the shed. "How's that?"

Axel grunted. He tipped his head back against the wall, catching a breeze off the weedy fields. When a parachute of seed fluff landed on his lap, he watched it settle, then brushed it off. After a while, he said, "We could go to Florida. We could rent a post office box and have the government forward our checks. We could drive right onto the beach and camp out." He looked at his father. "What's stopping us?"

His father picked up the posthole digger. "Not interested," he said. "Just the idea of a beach makes me restless." He lifted the tool straight up in the air, then plunged it down into the dirt and spread the handles.

"We could hire a boat," said Axel. "You deserve to get out on a boat. We all do."

His father set a post in the hole. "Maybe you didn't hear me," he said. "I sent this man money already. These animals, when they get here, are mine."

"That post," said Axel. "It's crooked."

His father straightened the post and toed a clump of dirt and gravel over the lip of the hole.

Axel said, "Maybe I'll go by myself, then."

"Not with Jenny?" his father said, kicking in more dirt and tamping it down with his steel-toed boot.

"She wouldn't take the time off," said Axel. "She'd rather shoot for her next brass plaque." He plucked a blade of grass and squeezed it between his thumbs to make a whistle. "Tell me something," he said. "Why would a man want to work and get rich if he never wants to retire?"

His father picked up the tool again and drove it down hard. "Talk to me when I'm done digging," he said. "That animal man could get here any minute."

HIS NAME WAS Mr. Rickles. He backed up his truck behind the shed, craning his long, scrawny neck out the window while Axel's father shouted directions and Axel stood back in the shade, observing, sipping some grape juice his father had brought him. Axel knew the man's name was Rickles since that was the name on the side of the truck, written in jagged letters meant to look like lightning bolts: *Amos Rickles' Famous Midway.*

Axel's father was walking backwards. "Easy, easy—keep it coming. Little to the right now."

Rickles stopped the truck a few yards short of the first set of pens. "This is fine," he shouted. "I start down that grade there, I'll never get out."

Axel watched Rickles climb down from the cab and shake his father's hand. Rickles had on work gloves and sunglasses. The arms sticking out of his red sleeveless T-shirt would have looked better with snake tattoos, since that's what kind of arms they were anyway, or so it seemed to Axel.

When Rickles slapped his father's back and got the same in return, Axel knew right away that his father had gotten screwed on this deal.

"Axel, meet Rickles," his father said proudly. "He's come in all the way from Mitchell, South Dakota."

Rickles held out his greasy glove. "Afternoon," he said. "You're the one who got poisoned, right?"

Axel looked at his father, annoyed, but his father was looking at Rickles, smiling.

"That's true, I got a face full," Axel said. "But that's all cleared up now." He didn't want Rickles to sense his weakness. He knew how these carnival con artists worked: they nestled in your soft spots, inserting their sharp hollow mouth parts and swelling up like ticks.

Rickles withdrew his hand and said, "Coming down your road just now, I didn't notice much cultivation. You boys just taking a break this year? Little time off?"

Axel's father shook his head—he clearly didn't appreciate this comment. "Not really," he said. "We're on Set-Aside. It's a program they have to give the land a rest."

Rickles looked out at what had been a bean field—Axel's best producer—and slid his sunglasses down his nose. "Looks pretty rested, all right," he said.

As the men turned their backs on him, heading toward the trailer, Axel went from embarrassment to nausea to anger. It was all intolerable suddenly, and he thought he would rather abandon the place than let it become an amusement for others. He pictured the tourists who'd soon be driving past, families from the city on their weekend in the country; how they would notice the huge yellow sign and slow down to gawk at the roadside attraction, a farm gone back to prairie, ragged with quack grass, and there—look, there!—an animal, grazing, a freakish donkey with stripes. Can't we pet it, Mommy? Can't we, please?

Axel stepped out of the shade, determined to assert his rights. After all, the property was his, even if it looked like no one's.

His father had disappeared inside the trailer; when Axel got up close and peered in, he could see the two men in the shadows, squatting, stroking something that lay on the floor of one of the rearmost stalls. Rickles was clucking his tongue and whispering, giving soft encouragement. His father was shaking his head. Whatever the men were stroking wasn't moving, not that Axel could see. Nor was the creature making any sound.

"What's happening?" said Axel. "Dad?"

His father looked straight at him, then away.

Rickles called down the trailer, "They'll be fine. They get a little sluggish riding all day in the heat."

Axel swallowed. "Is that the deer?" he said. "What is that?" He watched his father slowly stand, then move to another stall and bend down.

Rickles said, "They'll perk right up. Believe me."

Drawing on strength he knew he didn't have, Axel took an enormous breath and hauled himself up on the bumper. He held himself upright by sheer force of will as his vision abruptly reversed itself: dark things shimmered, light things dimmed, and what was far seemed near.

Testing his limits with every step he took, Axel finally reached his father's side. Things were of course much worse than Rickles had claimed. Squeezing into the narrow stall, Axel knelt down and laid his hand on the flank of the gasping brush wolf. There was more going on here, he saw, than just heat stroke: the creature was unpardonably thin and had either gone unfed for days or was host to a thriving colony of tapeworms. In any case, it wouldn't live long. Axel was certain of that.

His father licked a finger and dabbed at the brush wolf's mattered-shut eyes. "The others are just as bad off," he said. "I've never seen anything like it, never. Goddamn man is a criminal."

Axel stroked the matted fur and nodded. He looked around for Rickles and saw him down at the end of the trailer, smoking a cigarette, loafing. Axel considered telling his father to stop the check he'd written, but Rickles had probably cashed it already, and anyway, it was only money.

Axel said, "I'd fetch the hose, but . . ."

"You go on inside," his father said. He gently supported the brush wolf's head and it lolled in his palm like something newly born instead of something dying. "Honestly," he said, "just look at this . . ."

Axel stood up to go—there was his health to consider. He had pushed himself too far today and had stayed out in the sun for much too long. He did not want to leave his father's side, but his father did not seem able to move and Axel had to walk while he still could. He told his father how sorry he was, and a short while later, back in bed, turning on the farm report—corn had closed higher, but soybeans were down—he heard the old man's pistol booming in the trailer, aimed point-blank, putting the damaged freight to sleep.

❧

MY

HARD

BARGAIN

THE WHOLE WAY DOWN to Phoenix in
the car, my job was to tranquilize the dog. I hated the
feeling. First I had to pack the pill in a crumbly wet lump of dog
food, the way you'd hide a stone in a snowball. To get the pill in
tight so it wouldn't fall out or show, I'd squeeze the lump in my
fist for a second and sticky warm food juice would seep out
between my knuckles. Then I had to climb over the seat and get
my knees around Polly's neck, all without dropping the food. I
had to grab her bottom jaw and push back the gums and tongue
to work the lump in. She didn't like this a bit, and I had to be
ready in case she snapped. I had to clamp my hands around her

mouth and stay like that while she scratched the vinyl and tried
her hardest to keep her throat shut. I'd feel her starting to gag and
spit up, so I'd sing little songs in her ear to make her calm. And
every time I had to do these things, my brother Joey cried up
front, and Mom—whom I was supposed to call Judy because I'd
turned fourteen that year—stroked his hair and drifted toward
the shoulder.

That's why she let us eat junk food: to take our minds off Polly
in the back. The pills made Polly fart a lot, and she whined in her
sleep because she missed her master, the man who'd taught her to
hunt, my dad, whom I was meant to call Mike now. He was miles
behind us on the road, maybe even a whole state back, moving
our things in the U-Haul van.

"Kids today are so cut off," Mom said our second day out.
"Families are so much smaller now, so much farther apart. It's
really very sad. You don't even know your aunts and uncles."

"We've seen their pictures," Joey said. "There's Sam and Janet
and—"

Mom shook her head. "That's not what I mean. Now take your
dad's big brother—"

"He lives in Akron, Ohio," Joey said. To make him be quiet, I
grabbed his thumb and twisted. His habit of interrupting had
already hurt him in one school and I wanted to knock it out of
him before he got a bad name in the next place. Like Mike said,
Phoenix would be a fresh start for all of us; that's why so many
people moved down there. A desert is a huge opportunity.

I turned to Mom. Her chin was powdered orange from eating
nacho cheese chips. "We're paying attention now, Judy." Saying
her name made me gulp and blush, but Mike said it was worth
it—I'd find when I went into business, he said, that using first
names is the key to strong relationships.

"Look, we're in Iowa!" Joey said, slapping his hand on the

windshield. He was lucky it didn't crack, he had a ring on. I went for his thumb, he yelled, and Mom said, "Stop."

"You two settle down," she said. "Settle down or you'll wake your father's dog."

IT WOULD HAVE BEEN nice to drive in a convoy and stay at the same motels, but Mom and Mike got mad at each other the day before we left Wisconsin. It started when we were loading the U-Haul and some of the furniture wouldn't fit. Mike said we'd just have to leave it behind — two chests of drawers and the kitchen table — and Mom said if that was his attitude, that things were just things and had no meaning, that people were merely colored tacks you could stick wherever you wanted on the map, then she wouldn't mind being left behind herself. Mike said, "Well, you might have to be, honey," and though he said the last word sweetly, especially for a man so tall, she went on a rampage anyhow. She kicked a leg out from under the table and started pulling out drawers from the chests, letting them fall on the gravel driveway. I was inside the truck, labeling boxes with Joey. I told him not to watch Mom, just to label. I told Joey about attention spans, and how he hadn't developed one yet, which was fine if you lived in a town in Wisconsin where everyone knew your family and forgave you, but which wouldn't be fine in an Arizona city. By the time I was done with my lecture, our parents were talking and making up, sliding the drawers back in.

We ate a picnic dinner on the lawn, then Mike and I went to his den to pack his papers. There were light spots on the pine-paneled walls where his mounted grouse had been. "Wade, I have a proposal," he said. "If Polly rides in the U-Haul, I won't have the space I need to stretch out in. I'll pay you ten dollars now and up to a ten-dollar bonus in Phoenix to see that she travels comfortably in the car. To keep her from chewing the seats up, I bought some pills from the vet."

"You don't have to give me money," I said.

"No giving involved," he said. "I'm contracting for a service." He opened his wallet, wet his fingertip, and snapped out a bill. "As of today, you don't do favors, Wade. From now on, you charge for your work."

The lamps from the house were all in the U-Haul, so we went to bed the minute it got dark. We laid out parallel sleeping bags on the dining room floor and used a rolled-up rug for a long pillow. This is the way life should be, Mike said, and how it once was. He was talking mainly to me, since his bag was next to mine and Joey's was a couple of feet away, next to Mom's. They were talking too, about the Mormons. Joey had heard from someone that Phoenix was filled with the Mormons—he wanted to know more about them. I cocked my head to hear Mom's answers, but Mike's voice was louder.

"I like it without any lights," he said. "Electric power spoils people. There's no guarantee it'll last, either. It's purely a social contract. It's fictitious."

"It can go any time," I said, getting his point right away. He worked in insurance and knew the risk to things. Nothing stays how it is forever, and someday we'll all have to pay. He taught me that.

"All I ask of our family, Wade, is to see this move as an exploration. Traditionally in this country, when men have seen new markets open up—" He raised his head and looked across at Mom, whose hand was on my brother's forehead. "Is he crying?"

Mom said, "No. He's asleep."

"Joey, are you crying?" Mike asked him. Mike knew Joey was. "Uh-huh."

Mike said, "And is it accomplishing something?"

"Yes, it is," Mom said sharply. "If you cry when you're sad it accomplishes something. It accomplishes a lot."

"Answers my stupid question," said Mike. And after that, there was no more talking and we slept.

But sometime in the night I heard a sound. Two low voices, soft but angry, an argument of whispers. My parents were up on their elbows, fuzzy cutouts. The whispers were all about sex and checkbooks, that Mike was egotistical in bed, that Mom couldn't stick to a budget, that Mike's whole reason for moving us was to rip off senile retired people. The argument spread to other things, and I was hearing clearly now — without their bedroom door to block it — the fight they'd been having secretly for months.

Suddenly, Joey sat up in his bag — the whispering stopped. He rubbed his face and said the word "matches." No one moved or asked what he meant.

IOWA WAS HOT ALL DAY. Joey crawled into the back to nap with Polly, and Mom and I drank Pepsis from the cooler while she told stories about our family, the part that still lived in Ohio. The traffic heading south was heavy and made you feel a part of something.

"And that's how it is with all your dad's brothers, not just Uncle Ronald," she said. "They aren't your most caring people. They're also, when they choose, extremely fun to be with." She set down her can in the dashboard caddy. "Which isn't a widespread quality in Akron."

"But how did he *know* the cars were broken? Maybe he didn't know." This was back to what she'd said before: how Uncle Ronald had sold some cars whose paint flaked off when you washed them. He'd sold them out of his driveway, for cash, to people who didn't speak English. One man who had bought one tossed rocks at Uncle

Ronald's door, but Uncle Ronald never refunded the money. He called the cops on the man and scared him off.

"Oh, he knew they were faulty," Mom said. "You don't get four nice cars for what he paid unless they've got a defect. But the worst part is what he did with the profits." She checked her hair in the rearview, frizzing her bangs with her fingers, though it was only me beside her. "He spent it all on a party out at Firestone. One big night of country-club drinking to welcome me into the family, very flattering."

I barely heard her. Polly was waking up in the back, wrecking my concentration. I wanted the trip to go fast for her and knew it wouldn't unless she slept. I thought about the ten-dollar bonus for getting her to Phoenix happy, and how I'd be too embarrassed to ask for it. I'd never even gotten an allowance.

Joey's head popped over the seat. "Guess what she's doing again? Did you hear it?" He spluttered his lips on the back of his hand, making the sound. Spit went everywhere.

Mom touched her button and rolled down the windows, letting in Iowa farm smells. The wind blew Joey's greasy hair back into a crest like a woodpecker's. He saw himself in the mirror and looked like he liked it, an easy person to entertain. "I'm going to love it in Phoenix," he said.

Mom said, "Baloney, it's broiling there. The only people who like it are old folks, because they're cold all the time."

"Not the Mormons," Joey said. "The Mormons come to your house. They save you."

"Not you," I told him. "All that's gonna rescue you is homework. And you'd better do it down there, or else." I looked at Mom so she'd nod and he'd see her — he needed the reinforcement, Mike said. But Mom was facing away, out the window.

Joey smiled. "Mom and me have a secret from you."

"Since when?" I said.

He put his wet mouth against my ear. "She's already a Mormon."

Mom slowed down for the services exit. "So are a lot of people," she said. "Now who wants Burger King, who wants Howard Johnson?"

ALL THE BEST WESTERNS were full that night so we stopped at a no-name motel in Missouri. The office was just off the interstate—but when we walked around back to our cabin, there were cut cornfields running right up to the door. Out in the dark, under the moon, a combine harvester moved along with headlights as strong as a truck's. The driver sat up in a lighted glass cab that looked like a good place to be that night.

Our room was meant to remind you of Scotland. The shower curtain had men with bagpipes, the walls and bedspreads were plaid and smelled like pine trees. The ashtray between the beds was jammed with butts, and the first thing Mom did was dump it out and go to the bathroom to wash her hands. Polly slunk under the desk by the window and scared me by falling asleep without her pill. We sat on the floor with our bucket of chicken and watched the news of a town we didn't care about.

Joey got the rollaway. I got a bed.

Mom and I couldn't sleep—we'd drunk too many Pepsis in the car. I got out the atlas to plan our route and Mom set a paperback book on her lap that I hoped she wouldn't open. I'd already read it. Overall, it was thrilling, the diary of a French assassin, but there were some filthy parts, too. One description wouldn't leave my head: about the way a duchess's hair tumbled over her swollen nipple, and how the assassin bit her there and drew blood. I didn't want Mom to get to that part and view me for the rest of her life as someone who'd pictured an act like that.

She put the book on the night table, then let her head tilt back against the headboard.

"Kids don't have to know everything," she said. "I had my own life before I got married and it's my property. Do you understand that?"

"Yes."

"The fact is I *was* in that church, but only for a year, in college. They came to my room on campus, two missionaries, very good-looking. I was lonely, they cheered me up. Those Mormon boys, let me tell you, they're bred for their smiles."

I didn't say anything.

"But maybe you have ideas about Mormons. People do have those," she said. "That maybe they brainwash people. Your dad thinks that."

"I never thought that," I said.

"Well, don't. They're good people and they stick together, they call each other brother and sister. It creates a nice atmosphere." She spread her hands on the sheet and frowned at the chips in her nail polish. "My name was Sister Hansen," she said.

I told her that that sounded nice. She looked at me.

"Honey, it's after twelve," she said. "I can stay up and answer your questions, or else you can just believe me that this is not an issue for you kids. I'm not a Mormon anymore. Okay?"

We switched off the reading lamps clipped to our headboards and didn't wake up until nine. Joey was spitting out toothpaste in the sink while Polly lapped the toilet water. I hurried up pulling my cutoffs on, but Mom did something strange: she stayed in bed for another hour, too busy talking to throw off the covers. She propped a pillow behind her back and told us every last fact about the Mormons. She told us how all the men were called elders and had the powers of healing and tongues. That the church was run by a prophet who didn't get paid, that no one got paid, which was how it should be. She told us she'd been in a women's group that distributed food to the poor and sang at rest homes. And yes, she said, in Arizona there would be lots of Mormons, but she would be surprised if she ended up spending any time with them. It wasn't a church for modern women; it tended to stifle real fulfillment.

"I will grant you one thing," she said, though no one had spoken. "A person can get submerged in religion, lose track of her own opinions." Then she climbed out of bed and stood with her back to me, touching her toes to work out the night cramps. She changed her bra and fluffed her hair and bet me that Mike had passed us this morning because he was such an early riser. She told us not to waste time on showers and maybe we'd sneak up on him in Kansas.

WE'D JUST PASSED a sign for the world's best ice cream when Polly started to vomit. Joey was back there petting her, reading a book for once, and the vomit got on his leg. He yelled and threw the book against the seat—Mom swung her head around, I grabbed the wheel. Suddenly, there was a powerful car horn whose sound stretched out and got louder as a white Winnebago rose up on our left and walled off the sky, then shot ahead. Mom took back the wheel, angrily brushing my hand away. She looked straight ahead with a fierce expression and told me to climb in the back and help out. "I've had it with that animal," she said. "It shouldn't even be riding with us—that U-Haul had plenty of legroom."

Joey wanted to stay with the dog, but I wouldn't let him. Polly's condition was serious. Her smooth bluish vomit did not appear to be made of food, and the way it came up from her throat— silently, without any retching—made me think she had already died. I laid my hand on her ribs where I guessed a dog's heart was and felt a sudden, gentle leap of pressure, the way it feels when a hose is turned on. A fresh stream of fluid ran onto the seat. I lifted her head and set it on a bunched-up bath towel. Out the window streaked with bugs I saw my first-ever oil rigs, dipping and rising in the hot brown fields.

This was another country now. Iowa, Illinois, and Missouri had only been flatter Wisconsins, other farm states, and not worth paying attention to. But this was just grass.

For the first time that trip, Mom turned on the radio. I'd hoped she might pull over and hold a meeting concerning the dog, but when I heard the country music I knew she was aiming to drive nonstop until she had caught up with Mike. Myself, I didn't believe that would happen. He was behind us—I knew it—enjoying himself, taking his time between homes.

I could see him. He had on his Allstate Insurance cap, his belt with the Smith & Wesson buckle, his jeans and denim shirt. He'd set them out the night before we left, the same way Mom would have laid out a dress. Now Mike was wearing those clothes into truckstops, drinking cups of coffee at the counter next to the other long-haul drivers. He wouldn't feel afraid of them, either, no matter how loud or how big they were. He'd played offensive guard in college, and though he worked in an office all week, on weekends he lifted barbells at the high school. At a barbecue once in our yard, I saw Mike lift two women up onto his shoulders and spin around fast while they giggled and screamed and slapped the top of his head like little babies. Mom said not to watch him, he was drunk, but I didn't think so: Mike's balance was perfect. It was the spinning women who were drunk.

I raked Polly's fur with my fingernails, a feeling I knew she liked, and wondered if she'd shed her coat in Phoenix. I remembered the black-and-white picture of the house we'd already bought down there. The photo came from a real estate paper and showed a yard with gravel instead of grass. Mike said the gravel was different colors, only you couldn't tell it from the picture. Next to the house was a fat armless cactus that looked like a fire hydrant.

Mom turned her head. "What's happening back there, Wade? Anything?"

"She stopped throwing up."

"I suppose I should stop at a vet somewhere," she said. "Joey, honey," she said, "would you like me to stop at a vet for Polly? Maybe this is dumb of your mom, staying on the road all day."

"Mom, you shouldn't talk like that," I said, surprised at how angry I suddenly felt.

"Like how?" she said.

"That baby voice. He hates it."

Her eyes flicked up to the rearview, meeting mine. She stared. Joey turned a page of the atlas to show he hadn't heard us talk about him. Mom looked down at Joey, then back at me, nodding now and gripping her mouth tight, telling me I'd won some point that I would be held responsible for.

For the next two days we were tourists. We stopped at every attraction. Out of the car that first morning, Polly got some of her energy back—she pulled at the leash like her old self and even ran away from me once, jumping against the barbed-wire pen of the Texas Panhandle's largest longhorn bull. But by afternoon she was lazy again and she lay on her side in the backseat, slowly licking the vinyl, eyes closed. It was the heat, I thought. The bull had looked exhausted too.

Mom didn't bother to hide it: she was bored. While I guided Joey through the museums, teaching him about Indians and cattle drives, Mom hung back in the gift shops, buying things. All she wanted to do was waste time. She bought medicine dolls, wampum bags, anything they'd take a check for. The longer we were in with the exhibits, the more souvenirs Mom would have when we came out. But instead of showing them to us, she'd tell us how much money she'd spent, how angry Mike would be, and how little she cared.

"Anyway, we're about to be rich," she said. "All those old people *do* is buy insurance."

We stopped for gas that second afternoon in Tucumcari, New Mexico. The service station was shaped like a tepee and advertised genuine turquoise jewelry. Mom went inside to browse while Joey and I stood by the car, watching the attendant drag a sponge across our windshield. He asked us where we were headed.

"Arizona," I said. "We bought a house there."

The attendant frowned, making his bleached-out eyebrows touch. "Everyone moving down there now should have to bring his own water." He wrung out his sponge and walked around to wash the back window.

Mom came out of the tepee, stopped, held up her finger, said "Change," then went back in to get it.

"Your dog's not panting," the man said, pointing against the glass. "It ought to be panting."

"We know all about that," I said. "Just do the oil."

We arranged ourselves in the car, adjusting the sticky waist-bands of our underwear. Mom handed bags of potato chips around because we needed the sodium. Joey said we should go on a tour of the famous miracle cave whose sign you could see up ahead on a hillside, spelled out in painted rocks. "I'd just as soon stick to driving now," Mom said.

"Dad won't care if we go," Joey said. "We can do anything we want now."

After she slapped his face, after she said she was sorry and tried to kiss the red mark, after Joey pushed her away, she folded her arms on the steering wheel and put her head down. I could see inside Mom's blouse. Jiggling against her bra as she cried was a tiny cross, silver, with blue stones.

THIS WAS HOW it all worked out, how we came together again.

At six in the morning, one day later, we drove into Phoenix on the Black Mountain Freeway. Except for Joey, who curled up with Polly, we'd kept awake all night by drinking Pepsis, the radio tuned to a call-in show. It was broadcast from Salt Lake City, Utah, home of the Mormon Temple, Mom told me. But that was not why we listened. What made us sit up and shake our heads was hearing the personal problems of people nationwide. Lisa from Kansas City had caught her adopted daughter eating paint chips. Tony from the Bronx could not quit drugs and said he had sores on his arms. A girl who wouldn't give her name claimed that at that very moment she was alone in a public phone booth, counting some money she'd earned for having sex.

"What a night!" the announcer kept saying. "This switchboard's lit up like a Christmas tree!"

"And I moan and groan," Mom said. "With a brand-new home today"—she looked at Joey in the back—"and two kids with no cavities."

We entered the low-built, spread-out city along an avenue lined with palm trees. There were no other cars, just a paperboy riding a motorbike, and Mom said she felt like a movie star. She honked the horn and waved out the window. She told me she wished she had sunglasses.

The house seemed larger than in the picture, its gravel lawn was colored, all right, but the U-Haul was not in the driveway. We parked at the curb with the motor running. Mom closed her eyes and told me to go to the living room window to see if our things were inside. She asked Joey to stay with her.

They prayed together, I found out later. Without ever telling the rest of us, Mom and Joey had been doing it for months.

39

Mike was in there, sleeping on top of his bag in his undershorts. The room was a wreck, just filthy, wads of newspaper everywhere, a tilting stack of dishes, drifts of Styrofoam packing chips. The only clear space was the campsite he'd made: a toaster oven, a reading lamp, and a cardboard box for a table. He'd set out a plate, a coffee mug, and his red Swiss army knife, opened to the fork. There was no way to tell how long he'd been there or how long he thought he'd need to be.

I watched him straighten his leg in his sleep, then scratch his chest and roll over. I almost wanted to leave him there, to just go back to the car and say nothing. He looked like he wouldn't mind that, like it was something he'd already planned for, something he'd treat as a new hard thing to get through.

Then I heard the car doors open—Mom must have seen me staring in the window. She crossed the yard, giving me the "hush" sign with her finger. Joey was dragging the dog by its collar, slapping its butt to make it scoot.

But Mike was a hunter, you couldn't sneak up on him—he called my name and went to the door. I walked around to meet him, scuffing my toes in the purple gravel. He opened the inside door, but couldn't unlatch the screen half. He smiled at me while he fiddled with the latch. "You guys have car trouble?"

Mom, who was hanging back with her head down, lifted her chin and said, "Yes."

Joey let go of the dog.

Polly jumped up with her feet on the door and licked at Mike's bare belly through the screen, crowding the rest of us out—and though she was healthy only for that day and died under Joey's bed a few weeks later, I charged my father the whole ten dollars. After all, it was his own idea, me not working for free anymore.

᪥

THE

ORPHAN

W E'RE TWO DIFFERENT boys, no
blood in common, with only one set of parents: his.
Mine are out there somewhere, of course, but they move too fast
to be of much help now that I need help constantly. After my
junior year of college, once they were sure I'd graduate, my
parents sold their house and land and left on a never-ending
vacation. It started with a double tour of Europe—first the Great
Churches, then the Great Food—and picked up steam when they
went to Orlando and bought an option-packed RV, thirty feet
long, with cruise-control and dual antennas that rise up like
missiles when Dad thumbs a button under the dash. Now there's

no telling where they'll end up. According to my uncle, who keeps track, they live in the campgrounds of national parks.

This is a growing trend, I hear: seniors on the road. I saw a chart in *Newsweek*.

Kyle's parents are here to stay, though. They're people to count on, solid, and all you need for proof of that is one good look at their kitchen. All of their major appliances—and the Markhams own them all, from microwave oven to ice-dispensing fridge—are set in flush with the cabinets, as units, not like at my old house in the country, where everything ran off extension cords and looked like it might be gone the next day, tilted up onto a dolly and wheeled outside for the annual yard sale. My parents bought things used and sold them wrecked; Kyle's parents buy new, and send in the guarantee card.

The night I first set foot inside their house, the Markhams welcomed me into their family. Kyle and I had gone there for dinner because the apartment we'd rented that week still didn't have its gas turned on. We'd only been out of college a month.

"We see this house as a resource now," Mrs. Markham told me after dinner, settling back in her chair. "Richard, don't you agree," she asked her husband, "that Kyle and Wade, if they're smart, will view our house as a resource?"

"That's correct," Mr. Markham said. He wiped his mouth and put down his napkin and folded his hands on the table. "You see, Wade, it's not like when I was young. Everyone needs a network these days."

"I'm getting ice cream," Kyle said. He pushed back his chair and stood up.

"Honey, please, we thought we might talk now. All of us. Together," Mrs. Markham said.

"Go ahead. But I need ice cream," Kyle said.

Kyle's parents watched him leave the room. Their heads moved slowly, like video cams, then slowly scanned back to me.

"So, Wade, you're a farmer," Mr. Markham said.

I said, "My father was a farmer, yes."

"That's what Richard meant," Mrs. Markham said. "That farming's your heritage."

"Got that," I said.

No one talked for a moment—it hit me that I'd been curt. I tried a joke: I said, "If getting up at five in the morning and skidding around on frozen manure is what you'd call a heritage!"

I saw Mr. Markham frown. His chin formed little dimples, like a golf ball. He said, "You shouldn't dismiss your upbringing, Wade—I envy that attachment to the land. I'm sure our Kyle would have thrived on such work."

Kyle came up beside the table and stood there with his dish of ice cream, eating. I didn't like ice cream and Kyle knew it—that's why he hadn't brought me any. His mother accused him of rudeness, though, and instead of explaining the truth of the matter, which would have been simple enough, he told her I was on a diet.

She gave me a look of apology and said, "You should have warned me, I would have served fish. We're on a diet, too, Wade. Tell him, Richard, explain the program. Explain our longevity diet." I saw Kyle standing behind his mother, grinning. One thing he'd always said about his folks was that they had plans to outlive him.

"I'm glad we had the veal," I said. "The veal was delicious, really. Thank you. Thanks for everything."

"No problem," Kyle said. "Hey, Mom, you know all those board games in the basement?"

"Kyle, sit down," his father said.

Kyle patted his stomach. "Too full. Could Wade and I maybe take those games home? There's nothing to do at our place."

His mother shrugged.

"Thanks," said Kyle. "Well, Wade, you ready?" He sucked his

spoon, then set it in the dish. "I'd like to get back for 'Monday Night Football.'"

"Why not watch it here?" said Mrs. Markham. "Wouldn't you rather see the game in color, Wade? On a great big Magnavox wide-screen? *I* would." She smiled—I couldn't believe her teeth: a perfect set so straight and white she could have worn them as charms on a bracelet.

Kyle said, "Sorry, Mom, Wade has to work."

Kyle looked at me, winking.

I looked away.

I wanted to stay.

I liked those big TVs.

TWO MONTHS LATER, in August, the car I'd been driving to work—a junker Chevy my uncle had sold me for twice what he would have gotten from a stranger—ground to a smoking halt on the freeway and had to be abandoned on the shoulder. I didn't know what to do. I panicked. Kyle didn't have a car to lend me, my office was not on a bus line, and purchasing a replacement car was simply out of the question. Ideally, I would have had money saved—I drew a decent paycheck—but something about being out on my own, a full, free participant in the booming local economy, had got the best of my thrifty instincts. It wasn't rent or utilities that killed me, it was the little things: quality socks in every color, magazine subscriptions, designer frames for my glasses. Stupid things. The worst one was a certain kind of candy bar, Swiss, with triangular segments, dark and chewy, which I had tasted just once as a kid because they didn't stock them in the country; but now, in St. Paul, those candy bars were everywhere, calling out to me, dragging me down, making me eat at least ten of them a week at over a dollar fifty apiece.

The day after the breakdown, I called in sick to work and

stayed home with Kyle, watching TV. For lunch we had a cheese tortellini salad, a gift from Mrs. Markham. Anyway, it upset my stomach, and so Kyle took me outside for a walk, saying I needed air.

"Tell you what we'll do," he said. "We'll use my Visa to rent you a car. Pay me back whenever."

"That's forty bucks a day, Kyle. That's ridiculous."

"Then we'll just borrow my mom's car. Relax."

"What if one of your interviews pans out and you need a car for yourself?"

He shucked off the film from his new pack of Camels, the same brand I'd started him out on in college and then had had to give up myself when I saw the effect they were having on someone else.

Kyle said, "I never actually made it to those interviews. I should have told you, I saw this doctor." He blew out a perfectly circular smoke ring and poked it with his finger. "You know how I've felt so tired lately, really incredibly tired? Well, they tested my blood, Wade, and I'm sick. I've got mono."

He tapped off his ash in his palm and blew it into the street like a kiss.

"Mono," I said. "Didn't you have that already?"

Kyle said, "Not this form of it, this is new. It started in California last year and now it's practically nationwide. They call it the Screenwriter's Syndrome or something because it strikes the educated, mainly. No way can I take a job now. Really sucks, huh?"

I told him it certainly did suck and asked him to wait on the sidewalk while I ducked into a deli.

I couldn't help it: I bought a Toblerone.

"About the car thing, that's easy," Kyle said when I came back outside. "My folks can buy you a car. They'd love to. I'll just say it's for both of us."

He pounded his chest and coughed experimentally, hoping, I suppose, that something solid would come up. "My folks are crazy about you," he said.

He coughed again and finally got up some mucus, I think.

MORE IMPORTANT than mileage or styling, Mr. Markham told me, the thing to consider with cars was *safety*. We were standing in a rainy Honda lot, waiting to be noticed by a salesman. Kyle had gone to the office for water to wash down his antibiotics. Ten minutes later and still no salesman, Mr. Markham delivered a speech about the decline of good service. He blamed it on an erosion of values but didn't get specific. Thinking it was my fault that we were there at all, I asked him if we should leave; he shook his head. He'd brought along a paperback book that rated the major compacts according to their performance in crash tests. He was paging through it, finding the model he wanted.

"This is our baby, the two-door Civic." He showed me the rain-spotted photograph. "In theory, I'd prefer to buy American, but Detroit's so far behind these days in inner-frame construction—" He saw something over my shoulder.

"Kyle, get back in there! It's wet out here, you're sick!"

I turned around. I saw Kyle throw up his hands and do a fancy pivot, mock ballet.

His father closed the book and looked at me. "You kids don't share razors, I hope. Toothbrushes? Because you don't want to catch this virus, Wade. Bad enough that it went after Kyle. These modern bugs, they don't play favorites."

We found the right car without assistance, the only new Civic left on the lot. We opened the doors—they weren't locked—and climbed in. I sat in the driver's seat, hands on my lap, too embarrassed to take the wheel. When Kyle had mentioned the car to his parents, he'd said that if we didn't get one soon, I would have to leave our apartment and live all alone across town, where my job was. Leaning back in his chair, arms crossed, Kyle's father had considered this, then made his judgment: "That's simply not an option, Wade, splitting you two kids up. You're far too good for each other."

Mrs. Markham had agreed. "We have to stick together."

Mr. Markham was patting the gear shift, his wedding ring clicking on the plastic knob. "You any good with a manual, Wade? Ever use one?"

"Yes, I have," I said.

"Because if you haven't," Mr. Markham said, "an automatic's safer. That's what Rachel and I have in the Volvo."

"Either one," I said. "Whatever. It really depends on what Kyle likes."

Mr. Markham plugged in his shoulder strap, rocking forward to gauge its play. "My son is not a driver, Wade—he didn't grow up on a tractor like you did. I don't want him taking this car out alone."

It took me a moment to hear the command in this. "Fine. Okay," I said. "He won't."

BOOM, BOOM, BOOM—it happened that fast. First I received a ten percent raise, then, one week later, my boss took me into his office and fired me. He didn't give me any reason.

I never found out why I lost my job, and the mystery of it opened a hole beneath my feet—it sent me into a long mental wobble that made it hard for me to get up in the mornings and look for new work. Kyle's reaction only made things worse. Instead of giving me sympathy, he tried to recruit me into a club—the lonely rebels, the poets, the victims. He said we should move away to California and not tell his parents and live like bums.

I told him you needed money to live like a bum.

I'd had it with Kyle by then and he knew it. I'd had it with driving his father's car and letting his parents pay our phone bill. I'd spent the winter plotting my escape, a traitor at the Markhams' Sunday dinners, smiling as I ate their food but staring straight through them with X-ray vision.

But I was more dependent than ever.

AFTER A WEEK of unemployment, of watching my face break out in snow-capped pimples and letting my fingernails grow, I told Mr. Markham about what had happened. He warned me not to blame myself.

He said, "Take Kyle, for example, this virus. Ever since he caught this bug, I've asked him to take things easy and not get all down and blue that he can't be more productive just now. You see, Wade, with you always working so hard, it made my son feel guilty, understandably so. But what he soon learned—and what you're learning now—is that bad breaks happen. They do. As a farmer, you should know that. Would you blame yourself for a drought or a flood?"

"Probably not," I said.

"This will turn out for the best," Mr. Markham said. "You'll see."

We were sitting on his sectional sofa, watching the Twins lose to Oakland on the big-screen Magnavox. Kyle had fallen asleep in an armchair, not because of his "mono" but because he'd been drinking beer all afternoon. That's what he did with his days— drank beer and played with his stereo, copying albums onto tapes, which he put in a box and never listened to.

I dozed off on the spongy sofa and woke up the next morning under a down-filled quilt. Someone had taken off my shoes and slipped a pillow under my head. I spread my hands on the puffy quilt and watched them slowly sink, pushing out the air. I turned on the TV by remote control and flipped between cartoons. I wandered into the kitchen, opened the fridge, guzzled some orange juice straight from the carton. When I turned around to throw out the empty carton, I saw some plastic-wrapped melon next to a bowl of granola. Tucked under the bowl was a note.

"Enjoy your breakfast, tea is in the pot. Gone to the mall with Kyle to buy you kids an IBM PC."

A computer.

I didn't remember asking.

I finished my second breakfast, took a piss, and then, for no other reason than that I had the run of the house, I went upstairs with my cup of tea to see the Markhams' bedroom.

I'd never seen it before. It was gigantic. I sat on the bed and looked around. On the table next to the bed, in silver frames, there were photographs of Kyle, showing him as a baby, then on his first day at school, then riding a bike. In the last shot, he was a Cub Scout, aiming a bow and arrow at the camera.

Apparently, his mother and father had stopped taking pictures of him after that.

WORKING FOR MR. MARKHAM was not like working at all. The pay was good, the hours part-time, and for Kyle there was the added advantage of never having to leave the apartment. The computer sat in our living room next to Kyle's stereo and was linked by a modem to Mr. Markham's office in Edina. All that the job involved was inputting names and addresses obtained from various sources and collating them into specialized mailing lists: owners of pure-bred dogs, say, or Iowans with boats. Then you switched on the modem, entered a secret password on the keyboard, and sent the lists back to Edina.

It didn't upset me that Mr. Markham had never formally asked permission to make our apartment part of his office. What he'd done was install the computer, and then he'd suggested a few days later that if we wanted to, we could use the machine to earn some easy, tax-free money.

I did most of the actual work, while Kyle treated the computer as a toy. Sitting in front of it seemed to give him energy so I let him do as he pleased. Myself, I got tired at the terminal, the desk chair hurt my butt, and I couldn't stay at it for more than three hours a day; but Kyle, who'd always loved electronics, could sit there nonstop, testing new functions, playing games, typing away with his headphones on, absorbed. He joined a "computer pals" network that let him trade programs and personal stories with people nationwide. Sometimes he stayed up till three in the morning, "talking" with a Korean girl in Boise. Kim was a high-school senior whose family was very poor, Kyle said, and yet she had saved over two thousand dollars to buy herself a computer to help her with her science homework.

A month went by, then two, then three. I dropped my idea about moving out and finding a place of my own. I bought a cat with Kyle and fed it every day. And when Mr. Markham's birthday rolled around, I turned on the screen and plugged in the modem and sent him an electronic greeting. "Your faithful employee, Wade."

WE WERE OUT in the car, just driving and talking, laughing about something, when Kyle started to cough. The cough sounded to me like a bad one, deep and stringy. Kyle turned his head and raised his hand to shield me from the droplets.

I asked him if he was all right.

"I doubt it. This mono has cycles." He inhaled and his chest was full of whistles. "My parents think I'm faking."

I didn't know what to say to that.

He stared out the windshield. His jaw was set. "I was okay when I had those pills, but now, as an experiment, my mom and dad say not to take them."

He coughed again, bending all the way forward. "I got those pills on *prescription!* You saw the bottle—I had a *prescription!*"

I could see he was getting himself worked up now.

And then the blood came up. I was reaching for the shift knob, thinking that I should find a store where Kyle could get an aspirin or something, when suddenly I saw blood on my sleeve—fat red threads of it, like loose yarn. I couldn't take my eyes off the blood. At first I didn't know whose blood it was—I thought maybe we'd been in an accident. It was crazy. I checked the road to see if we were still on it. I looked at my sleeve again—then I looked at Kyle.

His head was tipped back against the seat and his hands were on his knees. A long twist of blood was hanging down from his mouth. The blood didn't drip, it swung.

I shifted down and took the next exit. I knew the route by heart. My goal was to get there before they went to bed.

I wanted the Markhams to see all this blood on me.

And then I wanted to be their son and live there.

WHOLE OTHER BODIES

I REMEMBER THE TIME of my family's
conversion, that couple of months before He saved
our souls forever. The nights I stayed awake too late in bed,
playing my radio under the covers, one of those midnight talk
shows with people calling from every state, a plumber from Utah
with cancer saying, "Hi, this is Don, I'm a first-time caller, and in
response to that doctor from Boston—" And hearing my parents'
bedroom sounds, their noisy bathroom trips night after night,
toilet flushes at five in the morning and someone slamming the
cabinet, coughing, spilled pills and my father cursing, kicking the
wall as they rolled behind the tub. I remember it as a time of no

food, nothing in the fridge, and then, the next day, too much food and all the same kind, cheese, say, pounds of it, but not any bread to put it on, my mother lit up in the fridge door, saying, "Cheese is the one thing you can't have enough of. This family *lives* on cheese." And how she would leave all the windows open and blame it on me or my brother, Randy, until we went over and closed them, but then in the morning those same windows, open again. Satan was with us then, I think, his spirit of confusion. Inside the house you could feel it.

My friends stopped coming over after school, I stopped letting them. What they might see. My father talking back to the newscasts, making fun of the president, or standing out on the porch with his drink, screaming out at the empty yard, "Of course no one listens! I've lost my voice!" And whenever the mailman came to the door with a box that wouldn't fit through the slot, I'd have to open it only partway, blocking his view of how dirty our house was, of dying plants that never got watered because my mother was always in bed. And sometimes I'd be mowing on weekends, cutting up close to the wall of the house, and I'd look through the window at everyone in there, sitting around the table after lunch, wiping their mouths with paper towels and not knowing what to do next, and I'd think: Too bad for them. Too bad for those sad people. But after my mowing I'd go back in and what I'd said outside would hurt me, I wouldn't like myself then, so I'd just watch cartoons or something, not thinking.

My father wasn't going to his job. He'd eat a big breakfast with Randy and me like he was about to go, he'd have on his watch and his best red tie, but the school bus would come and he would still be there, pouring new coffee maybe, and when we'd run out to the bus he'd wave good-bye, though he was supposed to be gone by then. Except that something was holding him back, making him lazy.

Only God could have saved how we were then. We had every-thing modern, sure, a phone in every important room, a new French blender, tilt-back armchairs with three positions, and no matter where you went in the house, even down in the basement, there was always some money lying around, all these extra dimes and quarters that you could just steal and spend on anything. But none of that was helping, nothing we had or owned. We were pretty helpless.

Then the missionaries came. They were there one day when I got home from school, two young men in tight dark suits drink-ing strawberry Kool-Aid my mother had served them. The living room chairs were grouped in a circle, so Randy and I sat down and joined in, a long conversation about Our Lord and his plan for the American family. The missionaries had short blond hair and slow western voices, their fingernails were pink and all squared off. They said they didn't mean to put us out, just wanted to make us aware of some things, and my mother and father smiled and nodded with wide, shining looks in their eyes, though their faces still seemed tired around the edges from so many months of trouble. The missionaries asked questions from a book, hard ones about the soul and where we hoped to go after death, then waited quietly with their hands folded while we all gave our answers.

The change was slow in our house and took a while to notice, our soft new way of doing things, with less bumping into each other, less noise. After their four o'clock visits, the missionaries left pamphlets and books, and my mother would open them up before dinner, asking if she could turn off the set because TV wasn't important now, its news had nothing to do with us—she'd rather go over the truths of the Gospel to calm our spirits before we ate. And my brother would do a thing he'd never done and kindly offer to get us all drinks when we finally sat down at the table. And I would pop up and help him, like magic, not feeling lazy at all, as though it was fun to pitch in and a very nice thing to remember afterwards, how I'd pleased my parents.

The missionaries came twice a week on old beat-up bikes with baskets in front, and one time they brought a movie projector and set it up in the living room, shining its beam on the dark wall where we'd taken down a painting of some dancers. In the movie they showed us, a panel of experts talked about decay, the decay of the nuclear family unit, just like we'd been going through, and it was a wonderful thing to learn that decay was happening everywhere, all over the country and all over the world, not just in our house. The missionaries were proud of the movie and kept leaning forward, pointing their fingers, saying how much we'd enjoy the next part because of its special message, and when the movie was over and Randy turned on the lights, the missionaries rubbed their knees and grinned because they knew how deeply we were learning.

One Saturday morning they took us to a park, me and my brother, no grown-ups. We had a picnic. The missionaries had made the food themselves: peanut butter and honey on white bread, celery sticks and pink lemonade, which they drank even more of than we did. The plan was just to sit under a tree and soak up the peace of sun and fresh air, and before we talked about God that day, they asked us about the sports we played, baseball and soccer and hockey, which were their favorite sports, too, and they promised to give us tips sometime. Then the tall missionary with the blonder hair told us about when he'd been a kid, that he came from a ranch with dozens of horses and one time a rattlesnake got in the stalls and he used a twelve-gauge shotgun to kill it. The other missionary talked less, just lay on his side sucking celery sticks, and every few minutes he'd pick up a stone and chuck it sidearm and hit the swing set where no one was playing that day.

My brother got sleepy from reading the Bible, but tried not to show it, being polite. The blonder missionary told him not to worry, to curl up and sleep as long as he wanted, we weren't going to leave the park without him. And while my brother napped on the grass, moving his legs in his sleep, we talked about whether the Holy Ghost could visit a person in dreams, taking the shape of an animal, say, or of a stranger, teaching truths that the person would wake up knowing. And we agreed that this was possible and might even happen someday to one of us.

I started to love the missionaries and so did my mother. She found out when their birthdays were, that they were both in June, and instead of having our lesson one night we drank chocolate milk and played a game where everyone had to wear blindfolds, which fit right in with my mother's plan to sneak outside and wheel in two new bikes, singing "Happy Birthday." The missionaries kissed her on the cheek, then on the back of her hand as a joke, while my father rocked in his chair and smiled. He was at peace like I'd never seen him, his face was smooth where it used to have lines, and I dropped my head to give a prayer of thanks, everyone getting down on their knees and my mother crying but not sad, a beautiful woman with wet cheeks when I secretly opened my eyes before "Amen."

Then it was time for us all to be baptized, a total immersion baptism in deep blue water. We wore white gowns like karate outfits, with loose cloth belts. The missionaries gave sermons first and everyone was there, the whole church, a hundred people from different towns who'd set up a table of cold cuts and cheese to eat at the party afterwards. And the sermons spoke of that perfect love which hovers around us always, in the sky, and of how some people ignored this love by always looking straight ahead with pinched, busy faces. But my family hadn't done that, we'd looked up.

One by one, we went under the water. First my father, my tall father, clean and pale as he held his breath and let himself fall backwards, braced against the missionary's arm. For a time his hair spread out on the water, then it disappeared, and that was the moment when God took him in entirely. It happened to all of us that day.

TOWARD

THE

RADICAL

CHURCH

He'd always liked motels even better than sleeping at home — they provided the essentials and left a man to himself; but in New York City they'd only have *hotels,* and Clarence Dahlgren felt confused.

The travel agent took time to explain the difference. She spoke with a sweet, exaggerated patience that said he should have known this all along.

"*Motels* are places off the highway. The name comes from two words, 'motor' crossed with 'hotel.' But they don't have motels in Europe, for example."

"Only in parts of America," he said, getting this straight.

"That's right. They're a New World invention."

Clarence nodded, licking his lips, then screwed them up into a confidential grin.

"Well, New York City's a new world to me!"

The travel agent coughed up a laugh that was almost shamefully false and returned to the arrangements, pausing over specialized terms as she would for someone new to the country.

"Now you're all set," she concluded. "Just remember to confirm your reservation the day before departure. Okay?" She slid the ticket folder across her desk and Clarence opened it, thumbing through each sheet of the carboned duplicates in the same way he counted money. That paper so flimsy could get you on an airplane moving five hundred miles per hour, this amazed him— almost as much as that something on paper could lose a person his farm.

NOW THAT HE'D ACTUALLY done it, accepted the church's invitation and picked up a plane ticket to show for it, people treated him differently. The situation was this: they were all in the same bad way out here, money and property sinking out of sight, and it just happened that this liberal New York priest had read a certain rural newspaper on a certain day and come across Clarence's name in the report of county court proceedings. There's nothing unique about Clarence Dahlgren, people said, he's only a representative, a type, and when he stands up before that congregation of rich New Yorkers he'll be just another hard-pressed farmer for them to clap at and cry over. This was the general theory that fall morning in the Taylor Place Café: I'm glad it's him and not me that church wants for its patron saint of bankruptcy.

At Rivard's filling station across the street from the café Clarence was heaving two oversized tractor tires out of the bed of his pickup and onto the gravel drive. He braced his hands on the side of the bed and vaulted down to the ground, consciously impressing himself with his own nimbleness and strength—something he did a lot lately. When the farm had started slipping away from him two years ago everyone had reminded him "at least you've still got your health." It had astonished him to realize they were right, and ever since, with all sorts of impromptu acrobatics, he'd held on dearly to the knowledge. Clarence was one of those midsize, slightly overweight men whose bodies you can't imagine under their clothes. But he knew well what was under them and was pleased.

He rolled the tires, one with each hand, into the mechanic's bay. The place did terrible work but held onto its dwindling clientele with an easy line of credit that had run the only competitor in history, a smart young man with a mustache and a General Motors Auto School diploma, straight out of town and back to St. Paul, where he'd come from with a wife and baby in search of sunsets and fresh air. The young man had had a reputation as a dreamer and an idealist—the names given to anyone who lived in the area by choice instead of inertia—but that was just why Clarence had liked him. They'd both considered themselves philosophers because of their foreign travel: Clarence had fought one war in Asia and the young man had fought the next one.

The tires needed extensive patching and that meant a half-hour wait for Clarence doing what he hated most: drinking coffee for the sake of drinking coffee, sharing complaints with the other men in the café instead of solving things silently in his own head, and then, when it was time to go, leaving a quarter for the waitress who'd done nothing to earn it but slap down a paper napkin and blow her cigarette smoke the other way. The men had already seen Clarence's truck through the café's window, so he had to stop in. He locked his back teeth to kill all expression and crossed against the town's only traffic light. He couldn't wait to fly to New York. Until he left he'd be public property.

Both the café and the filling station were going under—the cornerstones reading 1908 and 1922 would soon need a death date carved in—and the managements dealt with this by putting up more and more THANK YOU signs. Clarence pushed open a door that read THANK YOU FOR CHOOSING THE TAYLOR PLACE, never mind that it was the only café for ten miles. Glued on the cash register was a smiling yellow plastic face, and on the community bulletin board, pinned next to the softball tournament results, a poem by Anonymous compared "your patronage" to "the sun that warms the fields." Someone should rip that down, Clarence thought. If you have to beg, just come out and do it. That's what he planned to do in New York City.

"You're still not gone," the man at the end of the counter observed.

"I hope he's not keeping 'em waiting in their pews," another man said.

All the men looked the same. They wore shapeless denim trousers, work shirts rolled up to the biceps, and set down beside them on the dull Formica was a row of cheap baseball caps formed from plastic webbing, each with a seed company's logo sewn on the front. Some farmers wore these caps to keep off the sun, but some men truly thought they looked attractive and wouldn't go anywhere without them. The café attracted the second type, the show-offs.

"Let's buy you a coffee there, Clarence. Look tired."

"Thanks, Karl." Clarence stared at the ketchup and mustard, hating his neighbor.

"Julie," Karl said to the waitress he'd wasted the whole morning trying to make smile, "vouchsafe Mr. Clarence one specialty java and a sweet roll. Sweet roll fine, Clarence?"

"It'll do."

"Course in New York they'll be serving *croissants* for break-fast," put in another man, Pat Connors, who pumped sewers for extra income and called himself Dr. Shit-hole when he was drunk.

"And washing 'em down with champagne, I bet," Julie added with a sour mix of bitterness and longing. Last year she'd spent extra attention serving the Tuesday fish-fry to a man who'd claimed he came from New York. He'd left a fold-out strip of postcards instead of a tip. Every time Julie looked at it taped inside her high-school locker she thought of the story about dropping a penny from the top of the Empire State Building. "The velocity could kill a man," she'd heard, and she wondered why it didn't happen more often. Maybe it did and the news never made it out here.

"Is that right," Karl asked, "that they're putting you up and pampering you like that?" Heads turned.

Clarence steadied his hands on his cup before answering. Speak only kindly, he told himself.

"I believe they're concerned with my comfort," he said evenly. Julie snorted out loud, then tried to cover her rudeness with a little cough that immediately turned bronchial and messy. Her hands dove into her uniform for cigarettes.

"What I'll never understand," said Pat, "is why a *church* should be doing this. They're paying lots of money to see a real live farmer, that's odd in itself. But primarily: aren't churches supposed to feed the poor, not lay on political rallies? Correct me if I'm deceived."

"Since when were you last in a church, Pat?" asked a man who hadn't spoken yet. His name was Lloyd and he'd just sold Pat fifty acres to raise cash for a combine that hadn't run right from the day he'd bought it. "The thing is, Pat," Lloyd went on, "Clarence *is* poor and that church will be feeding him. So I'd say they're doing their job."

Pat wagged his head to show that such sarcasm was what he expected from a man of Lloyd's low caliber—someone who'd purchased a foreign-made combine just because it was cheaper.

"All I know, Clarence," Karl resumed, "is that you'd better put on a damned good performance to earn your keep with those people."

"As long as I get my point across," said Clarence. He wrapped his roll in a paper napkin and stood up with a senator's dignity.

After the meal, each man pitched in a quarter for Clarence's share and Karl swore he'd get his back some time.

CLARENCE DAHLGREN had two sons. Todd was a loss, brain scorched by drugs, but Joe was perfect— perfect in a way that couldn't last long, Clarence felt convinced, and once ended might leave Joe even worse off than Todd. It was Clarence's view that bad habits were better developed early in life when a man could still reform himself, rather than later on when the soul was less limber. But for the moment there was no reason not to enjoy Joe's perfection, his enthusiastic obedience and his smarts. These virtues made up, in the short run, for Todd's desolation: his car accidents, pregnant girlfriends, and the wor- ryingly constant supply of new twenty-dollar bills.

That evening, Joe stayed down in the milking parlor scraping the mucky concrete stalls with a tin snow shovel and humming along with the latest hits on the portable radio. He worked harder on what was left of the place than his father ever had. Disaster had bred a creeping sloth in Clarence, such that he didn't much care if the cows had to slog through their own piles each morning, but Joe had adopted adversity as a kind of stone to sharpen his will against. In his romantic idea of things, he was a prisoner of war grinning away under the boots of his captors—bankers, congressmen—and doing push-up after push-up to prove his unbroken spirit. The inspiration for this fantasy was a story Clarence had told about someone in Korea. If he had known the effect the story would have on his favorite son, Clarence might have warned him that the whole thing was a lie.

Clarence stood on the porch looking across to the yellow lights burning in the barn's basement windows and feeling guilty about how hard Joe worked for absolutely no reward. I should photograph him at his chores, Clarence thought, and project the slides on the walls of that church. That would make them feel bad, all right. The mist gathered at the bottom of the yard and the delicate evening sunlight fed his imagination. He pictured a stained-glass window devoted to scenes of rural destruction: haylofts gone up in flames, tractors sunk fender-deep in mud, wide fields shot through with hideous weeds and rearing black beetles. Above his head insects expired in crackling, violet sparks as they flew against an electrified trap, then wafted down as bug dust. A cinder stuck in Clarence's hair as he went down with the warm thermos to refresh his one good son.

Joe straightened up from his scraping.

"Tomorrow you're gone, old man."

Joe unscrewed the thermos cap and sloshed it full of hot chocolate. The boy hated coffee — an admirable quality in his father's eyes. Clarence associated coffee drinking with wanting something for nothing and lives wasted in talk.

"There's a good show on TV right now," Clarence said, feeling sorry for the way Joe rubbed his stiff back muscles. "It's all about animal courtship. You used to like those."

"I said I did."

"Oh."

"You should be packing your suitcase, Clarence." Joe always used his father's first name — a privilege he claimed in return for working hard. Todd wouldn't dare do the same.

"Already am packed."

"Good. Fine," Joe said. "Because we're all going out tonight."

"Who is?"

"Your whole family: you, me, and Todd's coming too. How long since you last hit the bars, Clarence?"

"My whole life. Except for one night I can't remember."

"We've got it all planned, the big send-off. Todd's bringing the van by."

The van was less formally known as the party wagon, and Clarence had never seen inside it, just smelled bad things coming out of it. But who was he to judge these kids he couldn't do anything for?

I'll kneel before all New York, he thought. I will.

THE VAN'S INTERIOR was a whole new world for Clarence. It reminded him of a whorehouse in Seoul he'd visited once on a dare. The seats and walls were thickly upholstered with a strange purple fabric that felt like the puppy fur on some Christmas cards. A deodorant stick hanging from the rearview mirror gave off waves of dying-lilac smell. There was a mattress in the back, and the whole place was littered with empty matchbooks, Styrofoam beer can holders, and V-shaped chunks of mud shaken from waffle-soled boots. Todd flicked a rag across a passenger seat and Clarence sat down while Joe climbed through the sliding door into the back. Dreamy electronic music played from at least four speakers. To Clarence it was all like being inside Liberace's stomach.

Todd warmed up the engine, slowly letting the gas through. He pampered the machine because he knew he couldn't afford to replace it. Whenever it broke down he'd curse the Ford Motor Company out loud; didn't they realize by now that some people have to live in their products? Todd had grown up having to sleep in the same bed as his brother—the van was the only private life he'd ever known. And because he'd arrived at this privacy so late, he overdid it. Some days, after especially long nights, he'd park at the scenic lookout in Siren Falls and sit with the tinted windows up eating potato chips and smoking and positively daring anyone to come up to the locked doors and check what he was doing.

Todd offered everyone cigarettes and everyone took one, including Clarence. He took one because Joe took one and he didn't want Joe to feel judged for it. Then Todd clicked down the automatic door locks for no other reason than to demonstrate his control over them.

"Here's our options," he announced. "Buy beer, drink it on the road. Or cruise to Wisconsin and take in the lounge act at the Bunyan House. Or else, if we're all in a driving mood, hit every place until North Branch and turn back once it's time. Dad?"

"You decide, Joe." Clarence counted on him to make the reasonable choice.

"I say, since Clarence is bound for New York to tell them all how we live out here, that he should make a fact-finding tour. So let's head to North Branch and hit all the stops."

Todd nodded and shifted into drive. Joe clapped his hands and whistled. Their father breathed deeply, searing his lungs on the unfamiliar smoke, and gave himself up to his sons' enthusiasm.

NORTH BRANCH LAY fifteen miles east, in the same direction as New York City. Todd kept reminding his father of this, saying that it was "ironic."

"You don't even know what 'ironic' means," Joe said.

The family had finished its first six-pack by now and things were getting lively.

"Like a coincidence," Todd said.

"That's how I always use the word," Clarence insisted.

Joe said, "The day you use a word like 'ironic' is the day your wife comes back from the dead."

The van swerved into the parking lot of the Palmdale Lounge, a prefab sheet-metal pool hall famous for fat tasteless hamburgers that looked even fatter because of the tiny buns they put them on. If you saw a man eating one more than once a week you knew his wife had left him.

The family walked in together, Todd in the lead because this was his territory. He'd angled the bill of his cap down over his eyes and tucked in his dirty blond hair under his jacket collar, but half the bar crowd recognized him anyway. Scrawny young men in sleeveless black T-shirts, whose stomachs looked sucked in to take a punch, called out Todd's name and clapped him across the back. For once, Clarence was glad of his son's notoriety—there was nothing worse than being the stranger in a room full of sinners who knew each other.

Todd showed his brother and father to his regular table under the TV set, then held up three fingers to a passing waitress. She winked to acknowledge his order and Todd winked back.

"Excuse me a second," Todd said to Clarence. "Got a tiny bit of business." He strolled to the bar and threw his long, starved arms around the shoulders of two pretty redheads. The girls leaned in symmetrically from their stools to kiss Todd's cheeks, then the whole group laughed for a minute—a happy, thoughtless laugh that said "here we are!" Todd jerked his thumb back over his shoulder and the girls turned two smiles on Clarence and Joe that were as fresh as peppermint.

"They're coming over," Joe whispered. "Just don't start buying them drinks. They've got a reputation for friendliness."

Clarence, already not feeling well from what he'd drunk in the van, took in the room full of young people with fish-eyed comprehension. Maybe it's time the farms should go under, he thought, because there's not a single person in this room who's fit to run one. But he couldn't say that to the church.

"Hi."

"Hi."

"Hello."

"Evening."

"It's Beth and Heidi," one of them announced, giving no clue as to who was who.

"We're sisters," said the one who might as well have been Heidi.

Joe said, "We know."

"Todd's great," Beth said.

"He is. He really is," her sister repeated, though no one had disagreed.

There was a short, smiling silence. Everyone breathed twice, Clarence the hardest.

"So, can we sit down?"

Clarence scraped his chair toward the wall to make space. With a single reflex the girls lit cigarettes, took one puff, then bowed to sip the drinks they'd brought with them, all the time keeping their eyes straight ahead and all lit up. Clarence tried not to look at them; their rouge hurt his eyes, too much and too orange—like the patches used on inner tubes. He watched another young woman, no older than these two, as she drank and talked and smoked rapid-fire, ignoring her tiny baby that was set down in the middle of the table, lolling in a stockade of empty beer bottles.

Joe was holding the girls' attention with a speech about the wasted lives of particular movie stars that showed an awareness of trivial detail that shocked Clarence. Maybe his son wasn't perfect after all. Maybe there was no one in the whole world capable of inheriting his farm, even if he'd had one to pass on. He drifted inside himself, his body felt heavy and old. Smoke chapped his throat, but the beer glass looked too far away to reach. His son, on the other side of the table, seemed miles off, impossibly tiny, and his other son had disappeared. Through a windy hole where the back of his head should have been Clarence heard a terrific swoop of rocket engines, then the squealing of lasers and explosions far out in space. The boy playing the video game swore when his planet erupted and kicked the machine.

What's to save? Clarence wondered. What's to beg for? There was so much he'd have to hide from that priest.

"To *New York City!*" Heidi's eyes flashed up from her compact mirror.

"Todd never told us that," Beth screamed. "That Todd!"

"Clarence is speaking before a church," Joe announced with a flourish of tipsy pride. "They want to hear all about our hard times back here."

"You mean the farm crisis?" Beth said doubtfully. She was quoting a phrase from the TV news that she thought applied to problems out west, in Montana or Kansas. "Is all that still going on?"

A hot jet of outrage shot up Clarence's spine. He saw clearly now what this room was full of, besides drunks: stupid, arrogant people who wouldn't admit they'd lost something until they woke up one morning in a ditch, landless, naked as fish.

"Our father says this farm problem comes from people buying on credit. People get ahead of themselves, then don't want to pay the price."

"Does your father own a farm?" Joe asked politely.

"The biggest around and still growing!" The sisters looked at each other, laughing crazily, orange cheeks bouncing. "You *have* to know Berrydale Farms!" Heidi said with the breath from an expiring chuckle.

Then Clarence saw what he'd so far missed and couldn't tolerate now: Joe's hand squeezing Heidi's thigh, fairly high up.

The bottle he swept off the table broke, of course, and Heidi's pink compact whizzed like a tiny flying saucer through the smoke before shattering in glinting splinters. No one even looked up. Beer slid down at its usual rate and pool cues stroked at the white ball.

Clarence jumped up, rocking the table, and Joe had to catch a beer glass before it tipped out on his lap. His apology to the girls was halfway between a grunt and a shrug. They might be pretty but they didn't deserve explanations. Then he followed his father out into the dark.

When Todd saw Clarence coming toward the van he ripped the money out of his customer's hand and tucked a plastic bag of grass into the man's shirt pocket.

". . . That's just how it is, I guess," Todd said, trying to sound like he'd just come to the end of a long conversation about something respectably philosophical.

"I guess so," Pat Connors said, catching on. "I guess that's so."

A thick, sweaty lock of hair licked across Clarence's forehead like a white flame. He fixed Todd and Pat in a straight-on gaze he felt sure would make them confess right away. He waited, giving them a chance. Above the group's head the rotating bar sign swept the faces with red and blue. Joe hung back in the lounge's doorway, watching.

"I hope you got your money's worth, Pat," Clarence said.

"You accusing your son of something?" Pat shot back.

"Not him, you. I know all about him. He's only making a living—you're the junkie."

"Not exactly," Pat said.

"You're the sicko. Todd's just an entrepreneur." Clarence's pronunciation of the last word was pure inspiration; he'd never heard French in his life. Pat's jaw tensed up and the muscles hardened in his shoulders, but there was no one here to fight. Just an old man, half-drunk, clueless about the modern world's workings and never likely to find out. Pat took a deep breath the doctor had taught him to help ease his ulcer attacks.

"Go to New York City, Clarence. See if you like it any better there. Hope you're mugged." Then Pat turned his broad back on the whole scene and started toward his sewer truck.

"You bet I'm going!" Clarence called after. "Those people happen to care for us — more than we do for ourselves!" The wind blew tears into his eyes and flecks of foam gathered in the corners of his lips. Todd reached out to touch his father's arm, but Clarence shook him off and stared across the parking lot and the dark highway as if he never planned to budge from this position. It was how he wanted his statue. The pedestal would read: CLARENCE DAHLGREN, THE LAST IN OUR TOWN TO TAKE THINGS HARD.

BACK IN THE VAN again, the sons had orders to continue east toward the next place. A change had come over Clarence, a thaw; he felt limber and all shaken out, full of the devil as he rode up high with the ground rushing under and his left hand wrapped around the whiskey bottle he'd guessed he would find in the glove compartment, and had. Joe wanted sleep, even Todd said he wanted sleep, but their father spoke with the true voice of excess when he told them: "Wherever we're headed, that's where we're going."

Todd couldn't help but kindle at such words, the kind he liked to hear coming from anyone besides his own father. Todd turned up the music and Clarence kept time with the drums, slapping the worn-out knees of his jeans.

"You probably thought I'd kill you back there," Clarence said to Todd.

Todd concentrated on the yellow line.

"Of course I wouldn't. You're just a victim! We're all victims! Joe, you know what I mean?"

"Yes, sir." He'd never called Clarence this before but he hoped the formality might subdue him.

"Victims on the run!" Clarence yelled, and he pointed his finger out the windshield.

Kneeling between the bucket seats, Joe checked the speedometer—65—then scanned the mirrors and windows for lurking Highway Patrol cars. Someone has to take care of this bunch, he thought. When the whiskey passed to him he tipped back his head for a healthy slug, then secretly spat it back in the bottle. But when the bottle came around a second time his father's eyes were on him, urging him, and Joe got so angry and scared that he accidentally swallowed off three inches worth.

Clarence asked Todd for a cigarette, lit it off the one from Todd's mouth, and passed it to Joe. Then he took another one for himself.

"Now the whole family's smoking," he declared. "See this, Connie?" Connie was his dead wife's name. "See what they've done to us?"

The family rode silently for the duration of their cigarettes.

"This van's not half bad, Todd," Clarence said. "You've fixed it quite nicely."

"Thanks."

"A mattress in back for sleeping—it's almost houselike. There's places to set your drinks, there's standing room. You've put in overhead lighting, carpet, comfortable seats. It must add up to a certain freedom, huh?"

"Guess it does."

"Park it wherever and that's your spot. Park in a field somewhere, you've got a place of your own. Home of your own . . ."

"Uh-huh," Joe said, wishing the man would shut up and drink more.

"This church that's invited me, that's what I'm telling them. Just that."

73

"What?"

"Buy us all vans. They're rich enough. Flying me out, aren't they? Must have cash to burn. They're renting me a hotel room, you know. European style."

"Todd, let's go back."

"Keep driving," Clarence said. He paused for a drink, dark trees sped by. "Here's my plan, boys. I stand in the pulpit, all those New Yorkers spread out around me in handsome suits and dresses. They're rich, we're poor—I make that plain with a few examples. 'The Bible,' I say, 'tells us we owe our neighbor. Americans might not like it, but you can't change religion to suit your continent. So give all you can, Mr. Lawyer and Doctor, hand it over to all us folks who are still having babies and getting up early and working Saturdays. Give us the money to save something.'"

"That's what you're saying then?" Joe asked.

"And I believe they'll be smart enough to agree. They don't want us in their hair and we don't want to be in it."

AT THE NEXT STOP, Andy's Sports Tap in Siren Falls, Clarence strode straight to the bar and took a stool in the middle. He hooked his toes under the metal footrest and spread his palms on the bar like they'd been saving that very space for him and he'd just come to claim it. When the barmaid, a girl barely old enough to drink there, wouldn't cut short her speech on the evils of duck hunting addressed to three men in bright orange caps, Clarence raised his arm at the elbow and brought down his palm with a stunning crack. Todd and Joe stared up and away at the TV set, ignoring the man.

"Three cold beers for three bad boys," Clarence decreed.

"All we got that's not out is Schmidt," the barmaid answered as if she expected him to curse this fact and depart.

"My family's too poor to make distinctions. Just bring something."

Todd reached into his shirt pocket for money, but when he was about to lay it down he noticed his father ready with a five-dollar bill. Clarence used both hands to smooth the bill perfectly flat against the wet bar as though he were pasting a photograph in the family album. When the bill was well stuck down he stared at it. Todd bit his lip and turned back to face the TV.

To Clarence's right a fortyish woman in fashionable clothes was picking through the contents of the purse she'd dumped out on the bar. Silver change had sunk down among the matchbooks and keys and makeup paraphernalia, and she fished out every dime to add to the stack next to her glass. Under her breath she counted: "Dollar, dollar ten . . ."

"How much was this again?" she asked the barmaid.

The girl gave Clarence his beer and his change, then moved down a step to help the woman.

"My vodka gimlet—how much?" the woman asked.

"You driving tonight, honey?"

"I asked you a simple question."

"One seventy-five."

"Shit."

The woman didn't have to ask him; Clarence had heard the whole thing. He nodded at the barmaid and pushed a dollar toward her like a real insider. For a long five seconds, she looked squarely at them both, Clarence and the woman, as an old priest might look at a teenage couple asking to be married. Then she smiled, shrugged, and took away the woman's glass to rinse it clean before filling it again.

"So it's true what I hear about country manners," the woman said. Her voice was soggy and tired, but to Clarence's ears, sweet. "Back in St. Paul you'd have moved down a stool."

Something told Clarence this woman was a professional, an

75

office receptionist maybe. She knew how to pitch her words so they slid under the voices from the TV set. He liked the effect.

"I'm sorry to hear that about St. Paul. I prefer to think well of the cities."

Todd and Joe couldn't help cocking their ears to this. They'd never heard their father trying to get in good with a pretty woman. Any woman.

"I'm Paula and I'm highly inflammable." Her vodka gimlet arrived, set down only a foot from her face; she nudged it back a few inches with only slightly chipped red fingernails. "They expect me to lean in and lap it like a dog," she said. "But that's only when I'm alone in my apartment."

"Just the word makes me feel lonely."

"Which word?"

"Apartment."

"Oh sure, like 'apart.' Me too."

The brothers nudged each other. Todd lit a match with one hand and they watched it burn down together, grinning.

"Which isn't to say I'm not curious," Clarence said with an upward sloping tone that usually preceded his speeches on abstract matters. "Apartments, hotels, people living like stacked-up dishes — it interests me. That's how we'll all live pretty soon. Your feet on my head, someone else's feet on top of yours, straight up into the sky until the air's too thin to breathe."

"That's horrible. You paint a miserable picture."

"Thank you. But you live in an apartment and you're a nice lady. And in New York City, those are nice people too. I'll tell you: if anyone saves the farmer it'll be the New Yorker. Because crowded people are thinking people."

"That's beautiful," Paula said, meaning it. She wiped her index finger around the moist rim of her glass for the musical note. The stranger beside her kept talking and she pretended to keep listening, putting in a few words here and there, but mostly she looked in the smoked mirror behind the liquor bottles and saw a man and a woman discussing, for once, something other than sex and who gets what. Wasn't that what she'd wanted from the last man—a little philosophy, some back and forth about things invisible? Actually, she couldn't remember. But this did fine, and the stranger bought her drinks too.

Todd and Joe had moved to the pool table across the room. Todd rigged the coin slot and they got three games for one quarter. They played silently, drunkenly, setting up overprecise shots they were bound to miss on the strength of other even harder shots they'd sunk by luck. Now and again they looked up to check on their father's progress.

"I'll never make it, you're right," Paula said. "It's fifty miles."

"Over fifty."

"It's just, well, everything you've said tonight. And this crazy dream of mine about waking up hearing chickens."

Clarence just said, "I know."

HE WATCHED PAULA'S headlights in the van's rearview mirror. They cut the dark like two white spears.

"Good to see she's not swerving much," Clarence said. He gazed sideways into Todd's eyes, looking for judgment and not finding any.

"It would be you that catches one," Joe said. "It's all that sincerity they fall for."

Everyone laughed. Clarence's share of the laugh was loud and falsely roguish—he swallowed it back when its meaning reached his ears. If a woman had taken pity on him who was he to pretend he'd seduced her? The ideas and words he'd shared with her at the bar came back to him cheapened, as though they were a line and not his real beliefs. The thought made him grind his jaw and sweat a little. He sat very still as he might under hostile observation and let his eyes inch up to the mirror—the lights were still there, thank God—before he glanced at Todd again, reassuring himself with the simple fact he had a son, two sons, that he wasn't a completely fraudulent person.

"Joe," he said, not sure what he was after.

"He's out cold," Todd said. "He's not a drinker."

Clarence turned and saw the perfect boy curled on the mattress, mouth open and dribbling a little, arms tucked up close to his chest, which rose and fell with sodden, uncomfortable breaths.

I could have saved the place, Clarence thought. When Pat Connors offered to take the eighty acres last year, I could have sold it and raised enough cash to keep the bankers happy a few more months while Joe figured out a plan. Joe's good at plans.

"Todd?"

"Huh?"

"That marijuana—how much money does that bring in?"

"Hardly enough to pay my transportation. I promise to cut it out, okay?"

"At least you'll still have the van," said Clarence.

The headlights had moved up nearer and Clarence watched them steadily now. He'd forgotten what the woman looked like, if she'd mentioned her job or not. He remembered something she'd said about loving the calls of chickens and he realized that she was the type who'd try to cook him breakfast in the morning and show off how well she handled the pots and pans. She'd stand on the porch and breathe the fresh air and go on about the scenery and the smell of frying bacon. He'd had one like that stay over once before when the boys were away at relatives. He'd liked the way that woman kept repeating how "lucky" he was to live in the fields and felt sorry for him at the same time, as was his due.

And tomorrow night he'd be in New York. No complications.

He watched the headlights; he imagined the packed church as he got up to speak. What had he done to be loved so suddenly?

Then the headlights flared in the mirror and the following car veered left and shot past the van, honking its horn, and then it was red lights Clarence was seeing, taillights.

B O A R D I N G   T H E   A I R P L A N E , Clarence was impressed by how many people could fit in such a small space when things were well organized. He took the middle seat in a row of three. The aisle was free but a businessman had taken the window. Over the man's shoulders Clarence could see the terminal building with other planes attached to it by elevated tunnels on wheels. Oversized golf carts with two or three trailers hooked to them snaked between the planes, delivering luggage and food. A man waved orange paddles, directing traffic. Clarence admired all this efficiency and wondered if farming would be like this someday: a tool for everything, many different workers, everyone knowing his job. No more wet mud in your boots and whole days lost from buying cheap parts for the combine.

Clarence noticed that the man beside him didn't bother with his seat belt and looked impatient to get in the air so he could flip down his tray and lay out his papers. Then the plane took off and the man did just that. Over the loudspeaker the pilot described their flight plan and Clarence calculated that the plane would pass over his county in a few minutes.

The businessman punched the keys of a small adding machine and began turning annoyed that he wasn't getting his answer. He switched off the machine and stared straight ahead at the seat back in front of him.

"Going to New York on business?" Clarence asked. He knew there were brighter ways to start this conversation, but he wanted to work up quickly to asking for the man's window seat.

"Business, exactly. Back and forth forever and ever. No use even owning a home with my job. Ten cities in four weeks. When you first start you feel powerful, like you could have a mistress in every city. Then you find out it would just be a hassle."

"Mind if we change seats for a minute? We're about to fly over my farm. I'd like to—"

"No problem."

Clarence settled in and looked down. He felt the businessman looking down with him, the breath on his neck. He didn't mind it.

"St. Croix River," Clarence said, pointing against the glass.

The recently harvested farms were black and gray and brown, with one white house apiece surrounded by a dark stand of trees. Some barns had tin roofs, reflecting the sun, others had dull-colored shingles. Clarence couldn't see people, but he hadn't expected to. The roads with cars were state highways, the rest were county and township roads. Working alone, the individual families had all done pretty much the same thing. The government's laws and the rules of finance and the practicalities of agriculture had made a landscape of soothing repetitions.

"Can you see where you live?" the businessman said.

"Not from this high up."

Then Clarence asked the man for a pencil and a sheet of ruled paper and began composing his speech.

THE

PERSONALITY

OF

WRITING

W HEN THEY FINALLY dispossessed us of the Warring Galactic Robots, everyone here thought it just went to show you, and now that we're sitting all in one room while we wait to see Dr. Erickson for our individual punishments, we can think of a whole lot else about Helping House that just goes to show you, so everyone's turning toward me and asking—since I'm the one who can chiefly write—"Why not standardize some of our history here on a big sheet of paper and send it to the newspaper or something? That way maybe the public at large can illuminate its ignorance of our lives here."

Of course I'm flattered.

Before I start, though, please comprehend that I am not like the others here. I work hard every day for my total regeneration. I don't smoke cigarettes and I never disperse my nontreatment free time playing the Robots, like Randy and Hem do. Instead, I read the *Science Made Simpler* books that used to repose on the Quiet Room shelves until everyone started maligning their margins with sketches of fang-faced babies and slime-bodied toads and other anomalous monsters. This malpractice has blurred my education. Now when I want to read at night, I have to ask a counselor for the key to our new security bookcase, and he will normally inform me that what I *really* want is another sleeping pill, which he is always delighted to give me and help me swallow. I could graciously write if they'd let me at the books more, but I can't in proportion to how often they won't. This is my valid excuse.

Anyway, while we're waiting for the doctor, I imply out loud to the group that they should originate several questions about our daily subsistence here which I will try to answer with my unique personality of writing. My friends are afraid to put names on their questions, but I wisely advise that it isn't our fault CPD's effects turned out to be long-term and medical instead of short-term and comical like we thought, so why be ashamed? In my own words that is what I say. My friends are awfully impressed by my sayings, and when that last one fully imprints them, they reabsorb their embarrassment and pass out some number-two pencils.

Peyton petitions: "Tell how Elton got sicker from Art Hour."

Here at Helping House, Art Hour is an expressive time for all of us. As the counselors tend to explicate it, the human personality inside us resembles a powerful liquid which can build up to toxic high levels unless we drain it off by making things. To discharge his own damaging personality, Elton liked to draw his dreams and fill them in with his lucky colors. His lucky colors were black and gray. Nurse Durbin, our rotating therapist, noticed this exclusivity of hues and pressurized Elton to try a few pastels. This would further realize him, she said, by making him more imaginary. But when Elton saw his favorite dreams in peach—the crayon Nurse Durbin cramped his fist around—he threatened never to sleep again, and when he finally did sleep, he woke up screaming. His condition continues to digress. Yesterday, when I looked in Elton's eyes, I sensed that his personal human fluids had drained away altogether.

Randy perplexes: "Why in the State Home aren't we?"

Elegant phrasing, Randy. You're improving. I will conduct my answer with reverence to my own experience.

I myself verged on the State Home once. One sunny, unremarkable Tuesday that I will never forget, my mother and father restrained me in the car and drove me there. On the way, my father proposed that mine was the incalculable sadness of leaving the School for Gifted Nebraskans. There was no way of telling, he told me, if chances I'd had there would ever be repeated. I countered him by forcefully inserting that kids like me who CPD had altered no longer felt at ease in that school where all the other Gifted Nebraskans were joined in caustic mockery against us. Truly reported, that was my eloquent sentence.

Once inside the mental facility, my mother toured the patients' cafeteria. Her air of disquiet was virtually breathable as she watched one bald and talkative young man reconstitute his peas and carrots. He mashed them into a colorful sludge, then smeared them on his temples with his fork. Once the nutritious balm had sunk in, his volubility peacefully ceased and his eyes slowly closed. My mother revolved on her angry high heels and led a family exit.

There are so many parents, she said in the car, so many just like us, she said to Dad, whose children used to be gifted, she said to me, that surely a nice private home could be purchased where

83

nothing like what we've just seen could happen. My father speedily agreed, but his was the responsible dilemma of wondering where to store his puzzling son until such an institution could be instituted. My mother upheld that my room at home could be staffed with a caring professional and emptied of any incisive objects that I might rashly impose on myself. All this was done. Snugly attached to my cot on the worst nights, free to sit up during others, I would remotely switch my TV to one of the speechless static channels and pass the hours connecting specks. After six long months of video isolation, I couldn't have been more pleased to hear that Helping House had been purchased and readied and that I would soon be mobilized there.

John beseeches me: "Tell about treats and tasks in the old days."

Gladly, John. It's what I'm here for.

Those were the days of the treat machines which we filled with quarters earned from doing tasks. Tasks were assigned according to what each individual did most pleasurably and least inadequately. John, who don't you be my case in point?

John's unique personality is based on a fear of glassware and ceramics. The story of how his fear came about is long and confusing and well worth repeating. John's parents left him, you see, before his formative years had fully shaped him. He was sent to a distanced uncle for further development. One afternoon, while John was alone in his uncle's apartment, he deconstructed the new color console by spilling a glass of orange pop down the slots in the back of the cabinet. John's uncle returned home to find the appliance inflamed. John was severely abraded for his mischief and he wound up in the hospital. When his uncle came to reclaim him, John escaped in search of kinder custody.

The people on the city streets were all the same in their indifference to John's flight. He worked odd jobs for grown men and was frequently brought to his knees. When he tried to get back on his feet by washing incessant dishes in an all-night diner, he was force-fed pills by the manager to keep him on his toes. One night, he overextended himself: his body fell subconscious to the floor, along with a tray of invaluable dishes. Swinging a whisk and a spatula, the manager reformed him from behind, then told him to scram, though John could barely walk.

A concerned socialist worker entered John in the foster-care system, but he proved to be unencourageable. He would eat only off unbreakable paper and he preferred thirst to handling perilous tumblers. The family court dislocated John to a long regression of foster homes, but his fear of domestic fragility only worsened. He turned to CPD for its illusion of solidity.

Here at Helping House, John's special task is the yard work. Lawns, being low to the ground, are highly stable, thus John's unusual fitness for the job. But now that treat machines and the Warring Galactic Robots are gone, John lacks slots for the quarters that kept him working. And all because of an isolated stabbing.

Arthur queries: "CPD is what? Tell them."

CPD is a drug that emerged from science to help large farm animals operate smoothly during childbirth and other routine traumas, and we liked it too. When you pour CPD in a drink and then drink the drink, you are in for some special effects!

We at the School for Gifted Nebraskans lost our gifts to CPD in exchange for sensations that no one can really rephrase. For me, the supreme distortion was manual, a loss of responsibility in my fingers.

One final note.

Dr. Erickson's door just opened and Randy came out crying. My turn will follow, but I'm not worried. When Peyton stabbed Nurse Durbin with the compass for making him rearrange his collages, I was alone in another room, practicing my future signature. As I stand up now, Elton is trying to write another question. He'll never finish. He holds the pencil straight up and down and works it very slowly, like someone using a screwdriver in an extremely tight place. I pass him and he tugs my sleeve, stuttering under his breath about injustice—a word I taught him.

Most of my friends aren't over CPD, see, and what they'll forever fail to comprehend is their failure to be comprehensible. Isn't that a nice sentence of mine? I couldn't have done it a year ago. But I've been working, studying, forming my personality of writing.

Too bad for everyone else here.

CONTINUOUS

BREATHING

RELIEF

T HE ACTIVE INGREDIENT in Vicks Vaporub is nostalgia. The stuff is medicine, sure, but when adults use it it's mostly a memory stimulant, and that's what makes you get better. When you were a kid you *had* to use it: a cool, oily mustache dabbed on thickly by your father. If the cold was a bad one, he scooped out a shining blob of it on two rough fingers and swirled it into your naked chest, putting pressure on the ribs and breastbone. The potion sank in, it really did, like saddle oil into a catcher's glove—you felt tenderized afterwards and petal-moist. You weren't quite sure how the stuff worked, of course, but your father trusted it and you had to trust him. Then he buttoned up your pajama top—the vapors had to be trapped to be effective—and got up off your bed, the absence of his two hundred pounds letting the mattress spring back to level. You knew that if you thrashed around too much, if you dispersed the vapors and didn't let them cure you, you would never make it to two hundred pounds. Your father switched off the light and left you lying very still in the aromatic, medicated dark.

"RUB IT ON ME," I tell her. I'm sitting up with a couple of pillows wedged behind my back, and thanks to my father and mother's care I've made it to *over* two hundred pounds. It wasn't like gaining weight—it was losing lightness. There were certain trees that I couldn't climb anymore, then none that I could.

"Come on, rub it on me for once," I say again.

This is my first apartment with my third serious girlfriend. She's only one hundred and five pounds—but then she didn't have parents most of the time.

"You rub it on yourself." She says this without looking away from the television.

I take my eyes *off* the television, I'm that annoyed. I'm ashamed too, just barely—ashamed for having expected something. In this mood I can't look her in the eye; I can't even look where she's looking.

SOMETIMES IN YOUR bedroom, with that cold, you coughed because you couldn't help it. But other times you coughed for effect, a little too thrilled by the sound's re-sounding. That was the part of you that wanted to die and your parents to find you, a pale, remote, angelic little corpse, absolutely not theirs anymore. You'd expired without a fuss, on your pillow, while they'd been upstairs lying like beached fish on their king-sized mattress, watching late night television. Now, looking down at your peaceful death mask, they'd have to admit they'd never understood you or properly loved you.

Except that you were a cowardly, selfish child, and didn't really want to die like that—no, you wanted to open your eyes secretly and catch them leaning over you, haggard with remorse. Then— maybe—you would open your eyes wide, startling them, and grant forgiveness. Or maybe not. If not, you could be certain the guilt and accusations would break up their marriage. Your father would move to town to be near his job, and take a vulgar furnished apartment. He would spend all night in the shadier bars talking to a bleached blonde with scarlet fingernails that she drummed, feeling bored, on the base of her cocktail glass as your father droned on and on about his tragedies. Your mother, she'd keep the house. She'd sort through your personal things, then carry them one by one to her bedroom like a robin retrieving twigs for its nest. She'd pile your things in a corner and waste whole days in bed just staring at them, smoking a cigarette and drinking sweet sherry straight from the bottle.

That was your power back then. That's why, sometimes, you coughed for effect—to remind yourself you had it. Even when the cough was sincere, a reflex, not a put-on, your sense of its power saved you from feeling *really* scared. Only once or twice were you so sick that you got confused and forgot to make things sound worse.

"VICKS ONLY WORKS if someone else rubs it on. The person's palm activates the volatile oils." I add this mock-scientific explanation to make my request funny and irresistible—and yet I actually believe it. The jar of Vaporub, still sealed, lies exactly halfway between us: a deep green amulet on plain white sheets.

"That junk soaks into the covers and stains them," she says. Her favorite character in all of television has just driven onto the screen. A woman detective with a masculine nickname, whose real-life pregnancy was written into the script last season.

My girlfriend admired that decision to let the actress keep working, and always talked about it as an example of real political progress, while I had no opinion. When she brought this up at parties I never argued that a pregnant TV detective *didn't* represent progress, I just had no opinion. But I did have a *definite* opinion about my girlfriend feeling so positive and approving: I thought it was very sad. Sad that out of all the grand inspiring things in this world for a person to admire, she admired *that,* something on television. What about Einstein? The National Cancer Institute? What about Churchill—or Gandhi?

That's how I put it to her one evening: "What about Gandhi?" I figured he was a safe choice given her politics and the kind of party it was—something on the beach.

"He was a man. I can't identify," she said, and the two girls nearest her nodded. It seemed to me she'd answered without thinking, though probably she'd done all her thinking on these matters in advance.

"I meant *Indira* Gandhi," I lied. My little trap for her knee-jerk feminism.

"She was a bitch."

So, you see, it didn't work. Her pantheon of the Truly Admirable was still pathetically empty, with a pregnant TV detective—and maybe the writer who'd found a way to keep her in the show—claiming the most prominent niche. And whenever that detective's program came on I'd make a point of reading all the way through and only half watching (the show isn't bad *dramat-*

ically), and my girlfriend would make a point of following the action so closely you'd think it was *Hamlet* she was watching. (To her credit, she loves Shakespeare—to my credit, I see his flaws.)

The important thing, though, is that now, while I beg her to apply the Vicks Vaporub and she ignores me for the TV, this doesn't signal callousness on her part or some Theater of the Absurd lack-of-communication on all our parts. The problem is that it is *her* show on TV, her genuine heroine; and on my side, Vicks Vaporub, especially withheld, seems the singular cure for a lifelong ailment.

I pick up the jar, feeling petulant and tiny, and read from the label.

RUB IT ON, USE IN STEAM.
RELIEVES DISTRESS OF COLDS.

Then in finer print:

For relief of head and chest cold symptoms and coughs due to colds, rub VICKS VAPORUB on throat, chest, and back. Cover with a dry, warm cloth if desired. Repeat as needed, especially at bedtime, to help get up to 8 hours of continuous breathing relief . . .

There it is, my trouble: "continuous breathing relief." That's what I need, what I don't have.

WHEN YOUR COUGH was croupy, like the lung itself decomposing, that got them scared, and your parents brought in the humidifier and set the portable television at the foot of your bed. Inside the humidifier was a plastic dish they filled with Vaporub. They turned the television on, but kept the volume low. They wanted you to sleep, but knew you were going to wake up a lot with such a cough, and the TV picture would be there to comfort you when you did. All these arrangements they carried out together, a single mind of synchronized concern, not like the times when it was only a cold and just one of them took care of you while the other one read upstairs. The croup was serious—a full recovery required a will to live. To strengthen yours, your parents put on a display of togetherness when they nursed you. They loved each other very much and you were loved by them.

Get better.

But when they left the room, your adventure was just beginning. It was late. The TV programs were all the ones you couldn't watch normally—a talk show, say, where a beautiful woman came on in a plunging sequined gown, sang a wild, throaty love song, then sat down in a row of chairs between the silver-haired host and a giant Irishman in a three-piece suit who glanced at the singer's breasts or reached over slyly with his hand and got it slapped. The host snuck cigarettes, palming them below the level of his host's desk. You never saw this man below the third button of his shirt. The desk set him off, kept him safe, while the guests were exposed full-length in their seats, wriggling and hopping under a weird, suggestive interrogation that was led by the host and picked up by the Irishman on the end. Everyone on that show knew everyone else. They were all each other's best friend, kissing cheeks, slapping backs, looking like they'd spent the whole last month in different parts of the country—New York, Las Vegas, "Tahoe"—and had just now come home to the only room they could relax in. What was so strange to you, seeing all this through the wobbly haze of humidified Vaporub, was that the room where these people felt most comfortable had only three walls. Any stranger could see in perfectly, and the people knew this and didn't mind. It delighted them. That was the phrase they always used: "I'm delighted to be here."

It was an enchanting spectacle and not quite real. The eucalyptus mirage effect distorted everything and your eyes kept watering. But the medicated vapors also drew the room closely around you; the eddies of aroma secured you against the greed and sinfulness that you knew were at the heart of that show which took place far away in Los Angeles, a city where no one had children, or stayed married for more than a year, or even went to bed at night.

Still, you wanted to go there. More than anything. Judging from the backdrop behind the host's desk—you'd never decided whether this was a painting or the real view from the top of the building where they taped the show—Los Angeles was a city of splayed, radiant boulevards fanning toward the infinite Pacific Ocean.

But if you ever *did* go there, you'd make sure to toss a jar of Vicks Vaporub in your bag, in case you ever got sick, struck down by the ceaseless, breathless chatter and all those late nights. And to remind yourself where you came from. That too.

W E ' R E   I N   L O S   A N G E L E S   now, my girlfriend and me, and that's why I can't breathe. She's from here so it's no problem, but I can't take the smog. My tender lungs, babied by Vicks for all those years, feel tense and fluttery. She knows this—I'll give *that* to her—and she's even learned a special massage at the Bio-Dynamics Center that's supposed to help. The catch is—and sometimes I think she exaggerates it—that Bio-Dynamics beats out most ancient *established* religions for orthodoxy and intolerance. Its key phrase, to quote the pamphlets she spends two nights a month tucking under people's windshield wipers, is "the abjurement of all Manipulated Substance and the wise exploitation of the Pure Element."

Vicks Vaporub is evil. She won't massage it into me. It has a petroleum base.

93

I'm handling the jar, fingering the metal cap. She's still absorbed in her program, its trailblazing sensibility, its pregnant detective. She's sitting straight, legs crossed Indian style, eating bran snacks out of the bag. Snap, snap—crunchy. Yum. I hate those awful saltless, sweetless things.

Now that I'm thinking, I hate this apartment. It's hers, not mine. In *my* apartment there wouldn't be that shitty batik wall-hanging. We're not in India—who is she kidding? We're not starving! In *my* place, if I could afford one, we'd have real paintings: square, framed, Cartesian, with people in them, or trees. We'd have a real bed, respectable and up off the ground, so you could put a table beside it with a lamp and a book. Like Americans have. And we wouldn't use this "futon," not a chance. It's lumpy, it was far too expensive, and I hate it.

I am really getting angry.

"Hey—"

She turns.

"My chest is pretty bad, okay?"

"Okay." In other words, What else is new?

"Can you just rub this stuff on me then?"

"I've told you I don't like touching that crap." (She models her hands on commercials—everything below her elbows is insured.)

Then, while she's still looking at me like that, I lob the jar of Vicks at her. If she catches it, that will mean one thing. If she doesn't, that will mean something else.

It lands in her lap, on top of the bag of bran snacks. She looks down at her lap like I've tossed a stinging snake there, astonished at first, and blank. But then—when the snake stings—she jumps up absolutely outraged and the bran snacks spill over the sheets.

Long pause. Then she makes a big show of taking a deep, deep breath. A deep Bio-Dynamic breath that centers her Cosmic Radius along her Terrestrial Axis, or some such crap, and proves what divine control she has of her emotions. When the breath

94

whooshes out—aggressively, obscenely loud for what she calls a "spiritual" exercise—she stands absolutely still for a second, gently shaking her free-hanging arms to get out the "negative energy."

Now she's pure; now *I'm* the asshole.

And next, as the angel of refined awareness, she softly kneels and picks up the scattered food, bit by bit, smiling.

Even the pregnant detective in a blind alley, with a gun shoved under her jaw by a maniac, doesn't distract my girlfriend's cool attentiveness. She slips each bran snack into the bag, stands up, goes to the kitchenette, and disposes of our little accident. When she comes back, I've got my eyes on the screen and the Vicks in my palm, safely cupped. It's a kind of just revenge that I've seen the dramatic high point of her favorite program and she's missed it, acting virtuous.

I am very angry. What makes the anger dangerous is that I feel every part of it, every corner, and I can adjust it—a degree this way, a few degrees that way.

"That was the closest your heroine's ever come to getting herself wiped out," I say. I support my words with five degrees of violence. I am precision.

"I wasn't worried for her," she says, resuming the Indian position. "It's a two-hour special episode and this is only the first hour."

I squeeze the Vicks jar, and I'll swear it's cracking. But what would happen if I just unscrewed the lid? The vapors are quick and volatile—they'd fill the room, they'd occupy it and surround her.

Instead, I cough. I start coughing. As long as I'm coughing I won't have to hit her.

W HEN YOU WERE YOUNG, in your small midwestern town or suburb, in your little blue room, late at night, with the croup snarling in your chest, your parents came in very silently and found the TV still on, playing a test pattern. You were sleeping. You'd kicked off your blankets in a coughing fit that had erupted in a dream. Your mother pinched the hem of your blanket and drew it slowly over you, up to your throat. If she was one kind of mother, she brushed back the sticky hair from your forehead and felt for a temperature. Hot, it was too hot. It was too cool.

Your father unplugged the humidifier and took off the lid. The water had all evaporated—to see you through the night he'd have to refill it.

"I'll put in more water, honey."

"Yes, Tom. Do that . . . put more water in."

"I will."

He filled the device from the bathroom tap. Then he scooped out a handful of camphorous gel and smeared it into the small plastic dish. His vision blurred, his hand had pins and needles, he had to work the next morning. He could hear your mother in the bedroom, adjusting the sheets. He wasn't about to complain.

He was married and that was his son in there.

He returned to your room and set down the humidifier on a table next to your bed. Your mother pointed the nozzle while he plugged in the cord. A soft, broad jet of medicated steam arced up and dissipated above your sleeping face.

"Good night."

"Good night."

They were whispering. They didn't want to wake you. It was a bad world they were preparing you for, but they wanted you to get better anyway.

⟡

THE

STEWARD

LUCKILY, I HAD A GUN hidden away.
It shook people up when I loaded it — an Ivar Johnson
twelve-gauge pump — but people would have been more shaken
up if I had not been armed that night. Without the gun, we would
have been helpless — just a bunch of dumb women, stupid kids,
and crazy old folks.

Except for me.

Dad was away on business and he wasn't supposed to get back
for a while. Mom was out cold on the couch and Grandma and
Grandpa were hogging the new recliners and playing along with a
big-money game show. They shut their eyes when the answers

were flashed on the screen and scribbled their guesses on cards, waving the cards in the air when they guessed right, but keeping the cards in their laps when they guessed wrong. The kids who were meant to see the cards and clap and feel proud or something were me, my little brother, and his girlfriend, lying on our stomachs on the rug. Boys Terry's age weren't supposed to like girls yet—my brother was only eleven—but Terry hadn't been acting his age ever since he'd started taking pills. The pills were meant to slow him down, to keep him from tearing around and wrecking stuff, and though the pills did slow him down in some ways, they speeded him up in others, like making him want to hug girls all the time and getting him so interested in math that he would cry and bite himself in class when the teacher didn't teach fast enough.

I ran to pick up the phone when it rang so that Mom wouldn't have to get up off the couch. Mom had just cooked fish sticks for the six of us, even though she was still feeling woozy from having her wisdom teeth pulled that morning. Her puffy jaw was turning purple-orange, the color of my little brother's girlfriend's makeup.

The lady on the telephone talked fast—I couldn't tell who she was at first. I think she thought she was talking to my dad, whom I had started to sound like that year.

"Deputies," she kept saying, "Indian. Deputies, roadblock, Indian."

"Who is this speaking?" I finally had to ask. "What is your business?"

"It's Janet," she said. "Mrs. Dilquist. I'm speaking to Robert Milgren, aren't I?"

"Hi, Mrs. Dilquist," I said. "It's Warren. Can I take a message? Dad's in Bismarck."

"Warren, put your mother on the phone."

"My mom's asleep. She's sick," I said.

9 8

"I'd like you to wake her up. It's important," Mrs. Dilquist said.

"I'm sorry, you'll have to tell me," I said. "I'm the one who's available."

I heard Mrs. Dilquist draw a long, hoarse breath, and then I felt a hand on my shoulder—my grandma's hand, her bad one, with the lumps.

"Who is it?" said Grandma. "Let me talk."

"Leave me alone," I said. "Watch your show."

But it wasn't any use. Ever since Grandma's friends had died and she'd stopped getting telephone calls of her own, she loved to horn in on our calls. She covered my hand with her hand, knowing, I guess, that I would let go of the phone.

I bet she knew I didn't want to catch her lumps.

WHAT MRS. DILQUIST was saying was that a dangerous Indian on drugs who'd probably robbed some liquor stores had been seen in a field on the Rundgrens' farm and everyone in the area should know. Anyway, Mom figured it out. She twisted the phone out of Grandma's bad hand and figured the whole thing out.

The first person Mom came to was me.

"I know this sounds crazy," she said, "but we should probably do something, shouldn't we?" Mom still had some laughing gas in her, or whatever drug they'd used to pull her teeth. Her words sounded chewed to me, and she was wobbling.

Mom stopped talking. She had to sit down.

She gripped the chair arms and tipped her head back. She closed her eyes for a moment. Then Mom reached two fingers into her cheek and pinched out a bloody, balled-up tissue.

Women can stand to touch anything, I thought.

"Everyone should go upstairs," I said when Mom was listening again. "Grandma and Grandpa have to go to bed. Only don't tell them why. I'll go get one of Dad's guns."

Mom just nodded. She set the bloody tissue on the chair arm as if it were something she still had some use for.

So far as I was concerned, Mom was out of it.

I DIDN'T HAVE ANY PLAN for defending the house. I'd tried to think of one the first time Dad went off on a business trip, but I couldn't do it.

Dad was a pesticides representative. For years he'd worked only the winter months and had farmed for the other three seasons. But then, last spring, he broke his arm, the farm got away from him, and he went to pieces. Our barn lost most of its roof in a storm and our new Dodge pickup dropped its transmission going over a wicked bump. Dad hung around in the house for a month, even after his cast was off, doing a Rubik's Cube in bed. He lost so much weight that it scared us, and when we could see all the notches of his backbone, Mom made him call up the pesticides people and ask if they would take him on full-time.

The pesticides people said Dad would have to travel.

Now he covered the whole five-state area, giving speeches at farm conventions and helping out with major sprayings. He hadn't expected to like the job, but now he loved it. "I found something out about myself," Dad told me. "I found out how much I enjoy meeting strangers. Especially when I can give them good advice."

Mom was glad for Dad, but I wasn't sure if I was. I'd liked things better when Dad was a farmer. Dad and Terry and I were a team then, all waking up at the same time, drying our hands on the same towel, then trooping out the door to work. Mom's name for us then was "you men," as in "Did you men wipe your feet?" Terry had been less hyper then, also — or maybe it had just seemed that way to me because we were outdoors all day, where there was less for my brother to wreck. Things had changed, though. Terry took pills now, Dad was always gone, and Mom called us men by our separate first names. Now we lived the indoors life.

The first time Dad left us, headed for Iowa, wearing a new green suit and lugging a case of pesticides booklets, he said he was off to conquer the aphids. Everyone laughed and wished him well, but lying awake in bed that night, I knew that our family needed a plan—in case there was trouble while Dad was away, giving good advice to strangers.

That's why the gun was under my bed now and not locked up in the gun chest in the basement. I'd moved it.

I couldn't believe now how smart I'd been.

I went to my room and shut the door and kneeled on the floor and reached under the bed, clearing away the sports junk and feeling for the gun. I broke it open and ran through all the safety checks, making sure that the barrel was clear and that the magazine was empty. I loaded three shells and put three more in my pocket. Oil I'd wiped on the Ivar Johnson last winter came off on my fingers. I covered my nose with my hand and sniffed.

Mom had done what I'd told her and sent Grandma and Grandpa to bed. I heard them in the upstairs bathroom, filling glasses of water from the tap to wash down their medication. I could tell they were taking their medication because I heard the alarm go off on Grandpa's digital watch. The alarm went off maybe six times a day, and wherever my grandparents were when it chirped—sitting at the dinner table, say, or playing cards with Mom—they would stand up without a word and go to the medicine cabinet, like zombies.

My grandparents weren't even people anymore.

I needed to piss from all the excitement, so I stood outside in the hallway with the gun, waiting for Grandpa and Grandma to finish what they were doing. Finally, I heard them shut the door that led from the bathroom into their bedroom. Dad had cut them their own private door because they had emergencies at night.

The bathroom was filthy when I went in. It reeked. You would have thought bums had been in there, or dogs. The towels had slipped down off the towel bar and the toilet bowl was clogged with paper that floated and swirled like a pink living thing. The dark orange water was almost over the rim.

I'd seen my grandparents' messes before, but this time I couldn't take it. I didn't see why I had to take it.

"Someone unplug this toilet," I said through my grandparents' bedroom door. "Other people use it too, you know."

"It's broken," said Grandma. "Go downstairs."

I stood there, both feet planted. I bumped the gun against the door to show that I was still there. After a moment, Grandpa said, "Your grandmother says she'll clean the bowl tomorrow. If she feels up to it. Go downstairs."

"She'd better," I said, "because I'm going to check."

Grandma said, "We'll see how I feel. I'm tired now. I ate too much."

This was the trouble when Dad was away: no one could make anyone do anything.

I thought about kicking the door wide open and letting my grandparents see me with the gun.

Instead, I just pissed in my grandparents' sink.

I ZIPPED MYSELF UP and walked down the hall to Mom's bedroom. Mom was in bed with her clothes on, lying on top of the blankets next to a mound of bloody tissues. My brother and his girlfriend had rolled out sleeping bags and were watching the new TV on Dad's dresser. When I sat down in the chair, laying the shotgun across my lap, Mom rolled over and frowned at me. "Warren, I hope that's not loaded. I'm not so sure we need a loaded gun. I think we can make our point with an empty one."

The news came on.

We waited for a report about the Indian. The news show came from St. Paul, though, far away, and the crimes up where we lived never got on it. The only way our county made the news was when the maple leaves turned red or when some farmer raised a record squash.

When the news ended, Terry and his girlfriend started kissing, right in front of me. They were using their tongues. I couldn't believe it. I felt like the man at the county fair who sits on a motor, gripping a stick, controlling the Spider Ride.

I felt excellent.

Then I heard the dog bark.

I stopped at the top of the stairs to check the safety on the gun. I saw that it was turned off, which scared me. Somewhere along the line I'd nudged the button, but I couldn't remember when. I shut my eyes and took a breath and tried to get my concentration back.

I pushed in the safety and went downstairs.

So many lights were on in the living room that the windows had turned into mirrors. All I could see when I tried to look through them was furniture and my face. I knew that someone outside could see in, but I didn't crouch down or hide, I just stood there. I raised the gun to shoulder level and swung it across the row of windows, picking out reflected targets — a painting of some swans, a plant, Dad's framed diploma from the pesticides institute. When I finally lowered the gun, I knew for sure that the Indian wasn't out there. He would have shot me already, through the window.

.   .   .

SOME TIME IN THE MIDDLE of the night, Grandma found me asleep at the kitchen table. She woke me up by asking if I was sleeping. When I opened my eyes, the first thing I saw was the sandwich I'd made after I'd gotten bored in the living room, waiting for something to happen.

"I put your gun in the closet," Grandma said. "That Janet lady called again. Everything's fine, she told me."

I looked up from the table. I felt woozy.

"I guess they caught that Indian," I said.

Grandma opened the cabinet under the sink. "All I know is the phone woke me up and the lady said everything's fine and don't worry, and now I can't sleep. Why don't you find the plunger, honey, and help me do some cleaning?"

"Now?" I said.

Grandma said, "Quit whining. Get the plunger."

I followed Grandma upstairs, not talking, and helped her do the toilet while everyone else slept. Grandma scooped out the paper from the bowl and dropped it into a plastic bucket. I poured the bleach in and did the plunging. Crud came up from the pipes that made me feel like I was going to vomit, but I didn't back off, I kept plunging. After a while, Grandma went to bed, but I had a motion going by then, so I went downstairs and cleaned the other toilet. By morning, I'd reached the basement. I heard people moving around upstairs as I worked on the pipe that led to the drainfield that spread out under the yard.

PAYING

MY

CALLS

Y<small>OU NOT ONLY HAVE</small> to meet the mother, you have to meet the mother's neighbors. You do if you're in England, if the girl you're planning to marry is English, if you're an American serviceman over there on a tour that's ending. I told Jane's mother I'd visit these people on one condition: that I could drink as much as I wanted and not have to wake up for church in the morning. Jane's old lady shrugged, she didn't argue. She wasn't in any position to argue.

Her daughter loved me and was sick of her and in forty-eight hours her daughter would be gone.

Jane and I went to the Bonhams' house first. They were nice people, maybe even the nicest in the village. They had the kinds of things in their cottage you'd probably want in your own cottage: souvenir biscuit tins, royal figurines, this and that from Africa. I held stuff up and turned it in the light.

"How much was this one?" I asked the wife.

"Six pounds fifty," the husband said. "That was back then, of course."

We sat around a low glass table, too low to be called a coffee table even, and smeared blue cheese on stale gray crackers and talked. Which of us really gave a damn? No one. But that's the tradition in England, you keep talking. Jane talked the least, leaving things to me, which was fine because I found the whole place fascinating, all of Great Britain, in a boring sort of way—just the way that makes for good talk with people like the Bonhams.

They asked me if I'd toured the country, seen what it had to offer, the variety. Had I visited Scotland? Wales? Had I been to Stratford? Cornwall? I said yes to these last two in a voice that warned them not to follow up. The fact was I hadn't been anywhere in England, except on base and in bed with Jane. We'd hit it off in a pub six months ago and had been hitting it off ever since.

"Where are you from in America?" Mr. Bonham asked me next. I watched his wife struggle up from her chair and take down a huge world atlas from the shelf.

"Duluth, Minnesota," I said. Really, I was from Taylors Falls, two hundred miles from Duluth and tiny—not a place they'd have found on their map.

The husband opened the atlas, holding it out so his wife could look too. "Minnesota," Mr. Bonham said. "Is that near Chicago by any chance?"

I didn't know why, but the man sounded hopeful.

"Actually, it's right next door," I said, lying again. I glanced at Jane, who was yawning, arching her back so a slice of tummy showed. She wanted to get out of England, she'd told me, because it was winding down as a country.

The husband rattled a page in the atlas. "Well, here's Chicago!" he practically shouted, tapping the page with his finger. "Chicago, Illinois, the Windy City. Home of many a gangland slaying."

The wife shook her head like that was really something, then took the enormous book in both hands and replaced it on the shelf. To discourage its use in the future, I suppose, she hid the book behind some tins.

The room got darker and darker. No one spoke for a while. I opened my mouth and started to speak, but the husband suddenly grinned at me in a way that just didn't fit with what I was planning to say. I forgot what I'd planned to say and grinned back. The wife shook her head like we were really something: her husband and the American, grinning.

Jane came in very politely to stop this. "You wouldn't have a drop of something, would you? Even a glass of water would do."

"How silly of us," the wife said softly, though you could tell she was panicking. "We haven't brought out the drinks yet, have we?"

When Jane and I tried to get out of that place, turning down a second glass of cloudy homemade wine, the Bonhams kept forgetting they'd already shaken my hand. I let them shake it over and over while Jane ducked into the bathroom.

"I assume you'll be buying a house with a sauna," Mr. Bonham said, finally letting go of my fingers. "I had an uncle spent time in America. All of your houses have saunas, he told me."

"That's true," I said. "They do."

The point of the evening was just to get through it, not to get all hung up on details.

On our way down the lane to the next place, Jane reached up

and straightened my collar, then made me hold still for a moment while she popped a zit on my chin. "You'll want to be in top form with this next bunch — they're rather upper-class," she said. "Not like the Bender-Smiths at the Hill Farm, but . . . ."

"The Bonhams seemed pretty upper-class," I said.

"Hardly," Jane said. "The Bonhams are teachers. They speak well, I know, but they both work."

That floored me.

"Michael, what is it?"

I pushed Jane's hands away. "Nothing. — Now there's probably blood on my chin!"

"Oh, quit," Jane said. "What *is* it?" She licked the tip of her index finger and dabbed at my chin, one of those tricks my mother used to pull that I'd enlisted to get away from.

"I don't like the way you said *work*," I told Jane. "We're not going to have much money, you know. I thought I made it very clear that you'll need a job while I'm in tech school."

Jane grabbed hold of my wrist and laughed. "But that's what I love about the States: *everyone* works, at least at first. And people don't hold it against you when you rise."

I let Jane kiss me. We kissed.

The Trumans' front door was open and Jane said we should walk right in, that Mr. and Mrs. Truman and their grandson would rather not have to get up. This didn't sound so upper-class to me, but it wasn't worth making some point of.

The old man and woman sat frozen on the couch with trays of those same gray crackers balanced on their knees. They didn't stand up to greet us, just stayed where they were and stared at their food while Jane pecked them both on the cheeks and introduced me. I had an idea that the room was filthy, but the curtains were drawn and there wasn't much light, so I couldn't be sure of that.

"Pleased to meet you both," I said. I would have held out my

hand for Mr. and Mrs. Truman to shake, but their hands were
under a blanket.

"Herbert!" I heard Jane shout from behind me. "You sneak—I
didn't see you." She crossed the room, arms wide: the grandson. I
could just make him out against the wall, a kid about Jane's age,
pale and scrawny, dressed in a turtleneck sweater that mush-
roomed out under his chin.

Herbert patted his knee and Jane sat down on it. "Good
evening, Jane's friend," he said to me. "There *is* a chair behind
you. Do make use."

I heard Mrs. Truman clear her throat as I squeezed myself into
the tiny chair. "We're all in rather a state of shock," she said.
"Herbert's letter arrived today. He's won a place at Oxford."

Jane let out a whoop and kissed the kid. The grandfather
sneezed like a kitten, *whiff, whiff,* a sound with nothing behind
it, no insides.

I had no idea where I was.

"Here's what happened," Herbert said. Jane was still on his lap.
"Grandmum here, who has a bit of pull, sent a note to the Trinity
tutors, *ordering* them to see me—"

"You little fibber," Mrs. Truman said. "I did no such thing!"
She paused, then chuckled, then everyone chuckled. I chuckled
last, distracted. The cane in my chair seat was starting to give—
under the chuckling, I could hear snapping.

"In any case," Herbert said, "the chaps did see me—"

The grandfather raised his hand, turning heads. "Herbert?"

"Yes, sir?"

"You're into Oxford."

"Yes, sir."

"So are a thousand other boys. It's not a thing to boast of, not
with guests." The grandfather dropped his hand to his lap as
though he'd had his say.

But I guess he hadn't. "Blacks and Pakis, Herbert, plenty of blacks at Oxford these days. You'll likely be just down the hall from some, sharing a toilet if not a bath. Not that you'll ever *find* them in the bath—indeed that's the one place you're probably safe. Blacks can't bear baths, ask the American—"

Herbert stood up. "I'll bring the sherry, Grandmum."

When Herbert had left the room, Mrs. Truman turned to me, smiling. "How *are* the American blacks these days? We saw quite a bit of them during the war. At dances and such. They were keen on dancing."

"Like damn bloody monkeys they were!" said Mr. Truman. He picked up a cracker and fiercely crunched it, glaring across the room at who knows what.

That's when I touched my thumb to my nose, giving Jane the signal for "Let's go." I'd worked this signal out with her because of all her snooty pub friends who liked to get on my case about NATO.

Instead of signaling back, though, Jane smiled at Mr. Truman and said in the phoniest voice I'd ever heard: "Did I tell you that Michael's family's in the hotel business, sir? You and he have lots in common. Tell Mr. Truman about your family, Michael."

I watched Jane fold her arms and wink at me, handing off the lie (the fact was my parents managed a campground, somebody else's, for lousy pay). Jane's tummy was showing again—I stared at it, wondering how far to go with this hotel bit, wondering what it was worth to Jane. I was just gearing up to tell the Trumans that my parents had owned a hotel *in the past,* when Herbert came in with a tray of glasses arranged around a dusty bottle that you could just tell had sat around for ages, getting more expensive by the hour. Jane got a pour and I got one and, suddenly, there was new life in the room and I didn't see why I shouldn't ride it out.

I'll tell you, though, by that fourth glass of sherry, with Jane in the corner egging me on, my lies got pretty wild.

J A N E   A N D   I   W E R E   D R U N K   as we walked up the hill. We started playing foot games. First, we played march-in-time, an easy one, but soon we were making up tricky ballets that tripped us up and threw us off balance, crashing into each other's sides. One time, Jane almost fell on her face, but I shot out my arm and hooked her back up. Another time, I fell, and Jane caught me.

"Where are we off to next?" I asked her, saying it the English way. I realized I'd never given England credit, but had mainly thought of it as a place to reinforce Germany from.

"We're going up," said Jane, talking in time with her marching feet. "Up, up, up to the Bender-Smiths'!"

I reached in my jacket and brought out the hip flask that Jane had shoplifted for me on my birthday. I took a short sip and Jane took a long one. She could be a wild girl sometimes. The first time I saw her, across that pub, her blouse was almost completely open and she was touching an ice cube to her chest, tilting her head back and sighing.

I don't care where you're stationed in the world, a sight like that jumps at you—you want to take it home with you.

"I think Mr. Truman liked you," said Jane, licking the gin off her lips. "Not Herbert, though. Old Herbert was jealous as hell, that brat. The moment he heard about your father's holdings, he started to chain-smoke. You notice that?"

"It's a miracle he believed me," I said. "Things got awfully farfetched in there."

Jane swung her arm around my waist and jerked me in close so our hipbones bumped. "*America's* awfully farfetched," she said.

·   ·   ·

JANE CALLED THE NEXT place a farm, but I didn't see any tractors.

I did see some swans, though. I did see a swan pond. I did see a horse barn that looked like a church.

And a house that looked like a castle.

With its lights off.

"Go ahead," Jane told me. "Ring. They're probably in back."

I rang the doorbell. We waited. My calves felt bunched and heavy after the uphill march. I shook my legs to work out the cramps as I glanced around at the palace grounds. It was nine o'clock by now, and dark. In the trees I could hear foreign birds start to call. Nightingales or something. Warblers.

"What time did they say to show up?" I asked Jane. She'd stepped off the porch and gone to the nearest window. She got up on tiptoes, grabbing onto the windowsill that must have been a foot above her head and trying to jump up high enough to see inside the house. Soon she was really struggling, really hopping. She looked so desperate I could hardly watch. She was trying to climb the damn wall!

Finally she said, "I'm seeing now. I'm seeing."

"You're scraping your knees," I said. "Come down." I walked around behind her so I could break her fall—she was literally up off the ground.

"Wait, I think I saw someone," said Jane. "I think I saw the maid. Try knocking."

I circled Jane's legs with my arms and tugged. "Come on, drop down. You'll set off some alarm."

I felt Jane's leg muscles tense, and then a high heel swung back and speared me in the belly kind of hard. I mean, I almost yelped. It really hurt.

"Hey!" I said.

"Let go," said Jane.

I cursed and took a step back. My dress shoes were sinking into the garden, probably crushing some priceless bulbs. "What's in there?" I said.

Jane didn't answer.

"Tell me what's in there," I said.

A few moments later, Jane said, "Empty rooms. Look out, I'm coming down."

My wife-to-be was crying as we headed back down the hill to her mother's house. I asked again if there had been a mix-up, but Jane assured me there hadn't been—that the people had said to come at nine on Tuesday. She told me that, as East Garston's leading family, the Bender-Smiths had an obligation to pass on their warmest best wishes whenever a village girl got engaged. "It's simply good form," Jane kept saying, blotting her tears with the heel of her hand. Another thing she said was "Someday they'll be very sorry," though how this would happen she didn't explain.

The moment we stepped in the house, Jane gave her mother a shout: "We're back!"

I heard some fussing from down the hall, and then Jane's old lady padded into sight, wearing a nightgown and fuzzy slippers. She looked like she might have been crying herself and had just now slapped on some makeup to hide things. Her cheeks were coated with dead-beige glop that formed little ridges under her eyes.

"So, it went well?" Jane's mother asked.

Her daughter nodded. "Very."

That surprised me.

"What about the Bonhams?" said Jane's mother. "They weren't too exceptionally boring, I hope."

"Not at all," said Jane. "Great fun, in fact."

That also surprised me.

"And the Trumans?" said Jane's mother.

"They were great fun, too," said Jane. She raised her chin and smiled at her mother. "They adored Michael."

Jane's mother reached out and squeezed Jane's hand. "That's so important, darling. —And what of the Bender-Smiths? Were they cordial?"

I turned my face to the wall, fixing my eyes on a painting there. The painting was of a fox hunt. Jane's mother's house was practically a cabin, only four small rooms, but every single painting showed a fox hunt.

"The Bender-Smiths were fine," I heard Jane say. "We didn't stay long, but they were just fine."

I heard Jane's mother say, "Good," and let out a breath she'd been holding.

There was silence.

Then Jane's mother said, "Michael, dear?"

I took my eyes off the bugles and hounds and faked a little smile. "Yes?"

"Thank you for paying these calls," she said. "It tells me you love my daughter very much and plan to live correctly over there. Poor manners will only hold you children down."

"Mother, we'll be fine," Jane said. "Tell her, Michael. Tell her how happy we'll be in the States."

Jane looked away while her mother eyed me.

"We'll be happy," I said. "Believe me," I said.

Though by this time I didn't know what to believe.

I had no idea.

A

SATISFYING

RIDE

IN THE

COUNTRY

I AM TWENTY-SEVEN years old. I graduated from Princeton with honors. I have a uniquely
challenging job. And yet the other day I decided to take an IQ test.

No one was forcing me. I had no plans to join the Foreign
Service, nor did I wish to enroll in a club for extraordinary
singles. I merely wanted to ascertain, in a private and reliable
manner, if there had been any damage.

My impression was that there had been some damage.

I found the test in the drugstore where I go to buy my magazines. Reading several magazines each week is part of my job as a
media critic. I am good at my job—I have my own column—but I

sometimes feel I should take more time off. When you cannot turn on a TV or a radio or pick up a magazine or even glance up at a billboard without having to come to some ultimate, publishable judgment, then consciousness itself becomes a chore.

I saw the IQ test displayed near the door after I made my purchases. A line from the test booklet's cover—"Rates ten different intellectual skills!"—caused me to smirk as I left the store. Ten minutes later, arriving home, I felt the smirk still knotted in my cheek. I wanted it to go away. It hurt. Thought followed thought, and that afternoon, as I entered some notes for a future column into my computer, I found myself reflecting back on all the illegal drugs I had taken. On how I had lost two sets of keys in a week once. On how it had been a number of years since I had divided a four-figure sum without the aid of a calculator. The next thing I knew, I was back at the pharmacy, buying the IQ test.

I HAD TAKEN an IQ test once before. I did not know what it was at the time: the booklet had no label. One day, when I was in seventh grade, the principal called me into his office, sat me down at his desk with a pencil, told me I had one hour, said "Go," and that afternoon, when I came home from school, my mother took me out for an ice cream and told me I was a genius.

"By two points," she said.

I finished my sundae and asked for another. Normally, I was allowed only one. My mother hailed the counter girl.

I decided two points was enough.

School became easier for me after that. I had been earning A's since kindergarten (or whatever marks they had given then—stars?), but I had had to work for them. When it was discovered that I was a genius, though, my teachers began to let up on me, assigning me "independent projects" instead of the normal home-work. In history class, for example, I was told to find the oldest man in town and tape-record his memories. In English class, instead of writing themes, I was asked to read two or three novels by Melville and give an oral report when I finished. At the end of the semester, I confessed to Miss Rivard that I had not read the novels of Melville. I told her they were just too long. She gave me a high mark anyway. I had become a school symbol by then, our chosen representative to Iowa-wide "achievement camps," mock United Nations sessions, and various other elite assemblies. For Miss Rivard to have flunked me, as I was well aware, would have been unpatriotic.

This pattern continued through high school. Oddly, I never had trouble with my classmates. Other, harder-working teachers' pets were subject to having their heads dunked in toilets or finding cat feces smeared on their lockers. But I was spared these attacks, I believe, because I never raised my hand in classes. My schoolfriends admired my modesty.

But modesty had nothing to do with my reasons for keeping my hand down. The truth was I had been excused from school for so many different camps and conferences that I had fallen behind in every subject. When I could not avoid being called on, I usually managed to last out the crisis by hiding behind "vocabulary words." If that did not work, I employed a technique I had learned while pretending to represent Ghana: I questioned the speaker's premise.

It worked. I graduated from high school one year early.

It was much the same at Princeton. I majored in English Lit with a minor in hallucinogens and scored top grades for "original thinking." For me, staying stoned was no handicap at college. Nothing had seemed real to me in years.

. . .

I DID NOT TAKE my second IQ test right away.

With the brown paper package tucked under my arm—the sales clerk had wrapped up the test like an item of pornography—I went for a walk to clear my mind. I watched a tattooed delivery man drop cases of beer through a hole in the sidewalk. I saw a girl in a Burger King uniform crying next to a pay phone. The steam pouring off the hot dog carts had never smelled more appealing.

But no matter how hard I tried to lose myself in reveries of ordinariness, the test remained under my arm. I could not shake it. By my third or fourth trip around the block, people were starting to stare.

You woke up this morning a genius, I was thinking—by two points. But what will you be when you go to bed?

Merely "superior"?

BECAUSE I HAD volunteered for this reckoning, I decided I had a right to optimize the conditions. I switched off the phone, I drew the blinds, I put a pot of coffee on the stove. I dialed the a.c. control knob down to a soothing, meditative hum. In hopes of re-creating that lucky seventh-grade atmosphere, I searched my desk for a number 2 pencil, preferably one with a slip-on pink eraser. What I found was a red felt-tip pen.

I scribbled on a pad and got pink scratches. The pen was dry. The signs had turned against me.

In the kitchen, drinking coffee, having set out the test on the living room floor, I recalled that my younger brother had said he would call that day from Iowa. Rick attends a state college back there. He is a drug-free business major, he plays on all the intramural sports teams. Every other Monday, he sends me his freshman essays through our modems, for editing suggestions.

I thought I had better call him to postpone things.

"Rick?" I said.

"Hey there, Paul guy. What's the story?"

"Why don't you send me your essay tomorrow. I won't be able to help you today. In fact, I'd like you to wait until Friday. I think I'm coming down with something."

"No prob," he said. "What's wrong?"

"Nothing—what do you mean?" I said quickly.

"Your voice. It's really alto. Pants too tight?"

"Listen, Rick." I cleared my throat. "I realize this is a personal question—but how did you do on your last IQ test?" I wanted to get an average family score, a kind of statistical comfort zone for later.

"Don't be dumb," my brother said. "After what you got on yours that time, I *know* those tests are bogus!"

"Oh," I said.

"Seriously," said Rick, "even the experts say those tests are fucked. It's just a myth that they measure intelligence."

"What do the experts say they measure?"

"Put it this way," said Rick. "You got one forty-five, right?"

"More or less," I said. It was more.

"Well, do you think I'm thirty points stupider than you?"

I paused before I said, "No." I shouldn't have.

MY FINGERTIPS STUCK to the paper as I folded back the cover of the booklet. Though it was called "The Original Cambridge IQ Test," the address of its publisher was Airport Plaza, Route 36, Suite 25, Hazlet, New Jersey, which not only didn't sound British to me or even faintly academic, but brought to mind a cinder-block motel. In one way, I welcomed this information: any hint that the test was not official gave me a built-in excuse if I flunked.

I turned to the instructions page and read the first paragraph: "What Does IQ Mean?"

Just as one's car cannot exceed speeds greater than its engine's horsepower allows, the human brain cannot respond to information greater than its own ability or capacity. Having an average IQ or inabilities and weaknesses in certain mental functions does not mean that one will have a useless and unfruitful life . . . *It is not necessary for one to push the accelerator of the car to the floor and reach high speeds to enjoy a satisfying ride in the country.*

For a moment, I saw that last image narrowly, picturing only the car, a station wagon, and I was all right. But then I saw the driver—his sunny, incompetent face—and I was not all right. The face was a blurry composite, and in it I could see fry chefs and clerks and losing game-show contestants and bowlers and men who operate snowplows for a living. I could see my own brother, even, and parts of my parents, the happy farmers—everyone but myself, the genius, zooming ahead in my lonely turbo Porsche.

I set the alarm on my wristwatch and turned to section one.

EXERCISE NUMBER ONE was worth an impressive twenty points. There were twenty numbered boxes, each one containing a different symbol—a dollar sign, say, or a circle. You were given exactly one minute to memorize the symbol-number pairings. Then you were required to turn the page and match each symbol with its proper number.

After a first quick scan of the boxes, I made a disturbing discovery: memorization is not experienced. There is simply no way to tell if it is happening. All one can do is stare and hope.

All one can do is assume one's mind is in there.

When a minute had passed, I turned the page. For whatever

reason, the cents sign, the dollar sign, and the sign for the British pound immediately called forth numbers. The various mathematical signs called forth nothing. Likewise, the shapes. I started guessing. Without any sense of how I was faring, I found it extremely hard not to cheat.

The rest of the test was much the same.

"THIS IS RICK DEMPSEY'S brother," I said. "I realize it's late, but I'm calling from New York."

"Hey, chigger!" the voice called out. "Your bro!"

I tapped off my cigarette ash on my slacks, then rubbed it in with the heel of my hand. I was sitting at the kitchen table, facing the wall. Whenever I let out a breath, the smell of vodka mixed with gastric acid rebounded up my nostrils. There was something I needed to tell my brother now that I had scored my test—I hoped that the drinking would help ease it out of me.

"Paul?"

"Hello there. Just a moment." I lit another cigarette and gathered in my glass and my bottle. "The reason I'm calling—" I said.

Rick cut me off. "You talk to Mom today?"

"No, I did not. Why?"

"You sounded weird this afternoon, so I told her to call you. I guess she didn't do it."

"No," I said. "But that was sweet of you, anyway. You've always been very sweet to me, Rick. Thank you for that."

"No biggie."

I heard my brother yawn then. I had to speak up now, before I lost him. "Rick, I need some advice," I said. "You remember when we were kids, and I was away all the time on those debate trips?"

"I hope you got laid," said Rick.

"May I just tell my story, please?"

121

"Thing is," said Rick, "I'm with a lady now. Could we maybe . . . ?"

"I'll get to the point, then," I said. I put down my cigarette and picked up my drink. "On one of those debate trips, Rick, I stayed at a Holiday Inn in Dubuque. I met a man in the lobby there who said he could get me into the bar. He told me he was a debate coach from Boston. I drank some Holiday Inn white wine with this debate coach from Boston."

Rick let out a whistle. "Pretty queer, Paul."

"Possibly," I said. "But that is not the point. He asked me up to his room, Rick. The man did. He sat on the bed and I sat on the chair. 'I want you to let me look at you,' he said. 'All I want to do is look.' So I let this man look at me—I was drunk. The man began paying me compliments. 'You don't know how lucky you are,' he kept saying. 'You're a handsome American teenage male. I saw you debate today and you were brilliant. If someone could guarantee me that I would be born again in your body and with your same intelligence, I would kill myself this minute. Anybody would. They'd slit their throat.'"

"What a fag," said Rick.

"You don't understand," I said. "The man was serious. He was dragging a cocktail straw across his throat."

"That's fags for you," said Rick.

I swallowed some vodka. "The man was sincere, Rick. People would die to be me—I *believe* this. I want you to tell me I'm full of shit."

"Be off in a sec," I heard Rick whisper. "Tell you what, now, Paul?"

Things had gotten too complicated. It was time to simplify. "I took an IQ test today. For fun."

My brother paused. "Oh yeah?"

"The score sheet said I'm a genius. I'm happy." I let this sink in for a moment. "Pretty superficial, huh?"

"Not at all," said Rick. "That's neat, Paul."

"Thanks."

"You bet. I'll tell the parents."

I let out a breath. "That's sweet of you, Rick. You've always been very sweet to me. And I want you to know that I'm doing fine here. Just a little tired today."

"Forget it," said Rick. "I'll give the folks your news."

I put down the phone. I sat there, shaking. I faced the wall and thought of Iowa, of its highways and seasons and churches and sky. I would have been happy to stay there, but my teachers and family pushed me out. They sent me out here, to the East, where the valedictorians battle it out so their lazy hometowns can have peace. And here I was. Trying to send home good reports only, lying to my brother.

The drop was of a mere six points, of course, but that is a lot when you are alone and have only two to spare.

DEVIL OF A CURVE

I N W I N T E R , the roads up this end of the county test a driver's character—go-getters, hustlers, and corner cutters just can't seem to stay on them. Crosswinds and heavy snows are the least of it, the devil is in the roads themselves. All those sleepy straightaways and views of scrubby, nothing hills, followed by piss-draining curves out of nowhere that strike on a grade and ice-plane the tires, and then you are skipping off into air, the steering wheel a plaything, there for fun. Most people freeze and hold a steady course, but some who have come to me afterwards for tows have said how the suddenly freed-up wheel was something they felt like spinning, and did spin, and these are the people who flip and fare poorly, at least in my experience.

I have opened my door on sights so ungodly gruesome and uncalled for that I have had to purify my vision by staring at a naked burning light bulb.

Generally, though, it gives me a kick, the fixes that people get themselves into, and that is why I keep the tractor all gassed up and conspicuously parked there. My porch light stays on from Thanksgiving to Easter, day and night—I tape the switch up. Last year, when things had been slow for a while, I went out and stood on the road, sighting back, and found that there were branches in the way. I took the chain saw to them and things picked up again.

Most people offer me money for my services. Without exception, I turn it down. Some of the drunks, the men, will go so far as to dump out their wallets or slip a ring off their finger. "Here," they say, sounding more self-disgusted than grateful. I hand them back their valuables and have them sit down while I heat some coffee. Often, when I get back to the table, the men are bawling, spilling out their sins.

They tell me where they were that night and why they should not have been there. With a teenage girl, perhaps, or running around with buddies while the wife was home alone. One man I had here a few years back claimed he had robbed a liquor store downstate—he even dialed the sheriff so I could turn him in. I wouldn't do it. Like so many others who've wept in this kitchen, the store robber spoke of his crash as a judgment, which I suppose it was.

That was back when my wife was still with me: she sent the man off with a bundle of tracts. Gail was Reorganized LDS, a purer strain of Mormon.

The only payment I do accept is the damaged vehicle itself. Quite often it's just not worth it to people to have a car repaired, especially when there are hospital worries. How much people waste has always amazed me—jelly jars that make fine little tumblers, pencils that are only halfway down, road-killed deer they could legally take home—but I have learned that you can't teach thrift. All you can do is soak up others' surplus.

Rarely do I sell my cars for scrap. The car I drive now, for example, is based on a '67 Nova chassis, with features from other classic GM makes going all the way back to 1950. Ever since I sold my livestock and got into Christmas tree farming, I've had some empty building on the place, so warehousing parts is not a problem. Still, it is probably time I rang the junk man: car parts today are not what they used to be, not so all-purpose and lasting, but good for only one year and one model—for anything else you're out of luck. It's just so hard to throw things out, though. You wouldn't believe how it tickles me, having some special part on hand for someone who busted it off in the ditch.

This girl who showed up last night, though, has not made up her mind—she may want repairs or she may want to walk from here. I'm in no hurry to make her decide.

VICTIMS HAVE STAYED overnight here before, and only once have I minded the company. I am not a judgmental person, but this man told me lies.

He stood on my porch for a while without knocking—I watched him from the upstairs window. He had on fancy ski clothes, brilliant purple, a color I suspect did not exist before this century. People in shock get confused, and that's how he looked: standing there in a whirl of snow, waving a snapped-off rearview mirror. His other hand was covering his ear.

Just as I reached the door, he knocked. Timid-sounding knocks, no more than taps, as if he had not yet decided whether he wanted aid. For a moment, he wouldn't speak to me, and I thought he was going to turn and run.

A handsome man with an ear streaming blood that I saw when he took his mitten away. I dabbed at his head with a moistened cloth and soon he started to talk, a mixture of nonsense and fine detail. He'd had a drink, he said, but only one. He hadn't been speeding. He loved his country. He loved its laws and had always obeyed them. All he'd been doing that day was skiing. Skiing cleared the lungs. He used to smoke. He'd cut it out and become an outdoorsman. He ran a corporation in the city. When I asked him his name as a test of shock, he changed the subject to Christmas trees. "I see by your sign you raise firs," he said. "Sounds like a very rewarding business."

"Mister, I think you're in shock," I told him.

"I am in shock," he said—a curious thing to say, if it was true.

When I asked him about his car, its condition, all he said was, "Write it off. We'd never find it anyway, it's buried."

Then he asked to use my phone, in private.

Later, I picked out his calls on my bill: one to our local county seat, ten minutes, and one to Minneapolis, twenty. One to the authorities, that is, and one to the people who own the authorities.

After he got off the phone, he told me: "I'd like to lie down now. I'm still in shock. I came to your house in shock."

Next morning, I found some change on the sofa. The man had disappeared. I drove my Farmall out to the highway, but just as I topped the hill before the curve, a deputy came running up and told me to get on back to the house, that the ditch down below was a sealed-off area, no matter that the land was mine. By now, I had pretty much guessed the whole story. The dead passenger, a boy as it turned out, was referred to in the papers as "the hitchhiker." The driver, "Milton Frick, philanthropist," had "fled from the wreck in amnesiac shock and collapsed at the home of an elderly farmer."

Cursing out the deputy, I started into a three-point turn. A

Cadillac stretch-job with tinted windows appeared at the crest of the icy hill, inching along for surer traction.

T H E   G I R L   I S in my son's old bedroom. I hope she has made herself comfortable there and will stay until tomorrow, when Tom is supposed to fly down for the holidays. The truth is it's more of a girl's room than a boy's room—all those religious samplers on the walls, a bedspread alive with Bible scenes.

Like me, my wife was hoping for a boy. The conflict between us lay elsewhere, in the kind of boy we hoped for. Except for wanting average size and weight, I had no specific expectations. But Gail had a child prophet in mind, a second Joseph Smith. She wanted a fairy who spoke in tongues, a scholar.

He had to be pure, so she bought him stiff white shirts. Even outdoors in the fields with me he had to wear a collar. Otherwise, she wouldn't fix his lunch. He wasn't allowed to drink coffee or tea or watch TV outside of the news shows. Gail approved of the news shows because she thought they proved to Tom how near the Second Coming was, so many wars and storms. I should have spoken up, but I kept quiet. The boy was on her side, not mine. The only togetherness Tom and I had was hauling wrecked cars out of snowbanks, a job that would fascinate any young man.

Tom made his mother proud with his faith, but when she died he lost it, fast. At eighteen years old he moved to Alaska, swearing it was money from now on, nothing for him but countable cash. He has a job in oil now, and tells me he could retire if he chose, that's how rich he is. He writes me downhearted letters sometimes, complaining that he's missed so much of life and that there are no nice women up there.

Well, I have a nice one here with me now, and I think my son would like her. I found her in the ditch.

JULIE, THE GIRL, sits down to eat breakfast. The sweater I gave her last night in the snow is wrapped around her shoulders, cute. This will be the first square meal she's had here.

She's already told me a lot about herself: that she has a problem with drugs, cocaine, and that she was driving stoned at the time; that her family, what's left of it, lives off a fund established by her grandpa, an engineer with a bolt named after him; that she was in college until last month, but left when she took her first exam and realized she was being timed. She tells me that what she hates most is time, not just clocks, but Time. She calls it an aggressive male invention.

What's odd is that she told me all these things before we had made it back to the house, while we were still on the tractor, towing. Julie is a talker.

"What do you want with your eggs?" I say. "Sausage or bacon?"

"I'm sorry, I don't eat red meat," she says.

"Pork isn't red," I tell her.

"Yes it is."

I am the farmer here, but why begin the morning with a quarrel?

"Do you mind if I smoke at the table?" she asks.

"Be my guest," I tell her. I'm amazed that she still has her cigarettes; I had to drag her out through the window, her car was that submerged.

Julie smokes, I eat. We both drink coffee. She asks me about my Christmas trees. I tell her that in the seventies the market for real trees bottomed out and I went hungry for three seasons running. Everyone wanted aluminum then, a clean decoration that doesn't shed. But then, when Reagan got in, I tell her—strangely, she still appears to be listening—real trees came back with a vengeance. Business has been healthy ever since.

"It just goes to show you," Julie says, laughing. "Fascism always—" She stops. She regards her long ash and frowns. "I really shot off my mouth last night, didn't I? Maybe I said some things I shouldn't have."

"Forget it, you were in shock," I tell her. "Now what was this about trees and Hitler?" I don't want Julie to lose momentum—it's sixteen long hours till Tom gets home.

"Nothing," she says. "I'm full of shit. I've never even held a job, you know that?"

"You're a girl," I say. "That's natural."

Julie looks away from me.

"Listen," I say after too much silence. "You want some cocaine? I dug some out of a car seat once—I'll bet it's still around here somewhere."

IT ISN'T LIKE ME to get my hopes up, not when other people are involved. By five in the evening, with Julie long gone—a girlfriend from the city came and got her, they took away a six-foot tree—I am ready to live without hopes forever, hopes of any kind.

What am I so in need of anyway? Not a thing. The world as it is brings bounty to my doorstep.

After a lot of tricky prying, I manage to raise the hood on Julie's Escort. I hook my shop lamp into the grille. The car is mine, she told me, so long as I talk up the damage level when her insurance agent calls. Still, I'm not sure if I want this car, even for parts. Too tinny. A twig not even as thick as my finger is rammed straight through the radiator, that's the quality metal we're talking.

Just working in the shop is soothing, though, and so I get my jack out, pump the handle. It makes me feel strong to raise a car this light. What you can lift, huh? That's what shows you. Once, I could lift my wife and my son, one on either shoulder. Then it was just my wife. Then it was only the smaller firs. Now, I have people cut the trees themselves, I let them make an adventure out of it. They seem to prefer it this way, tramping along through the snow with their saws.

I get the car up.

I shouldn't already be dizzy, but I am, and now I can feel myself breaking my vow and giving in to hope.

A boy showed up at my door one night, a school friend of Tom's—I recognized the jacket. His face was another story, however. No one would have recognized that face: too much glass and blood, too little hair. One of his eyes was all puffed shut, the healthy one. I must have made some noise when I first saw him, because my son called down the stairs then, asking what was wrong. I yelled at his mother to keep him up there, one of the few commands I ever gave her. Now that Tom is grown, though, I think he could stand to see it all—I hope he comes down from Alaska for good.

I won't be around forever, I'll tell him, and someone has to watch over that curve.

꙱

THE

NEW

TIMOTHY

W HEN THE OLDER BOYS in our
ward came home from their two-year missions to
Panama or Guam or wherever the men in Salt Lake had sent them,
the first things they usually wanted to do were not the things you'd
think, such as date girls and grow out their buzz cuts. Not for the
first few weeks, at least. The boys had grown into statesmen while
abroad, diplomats of the Gospel, and what they wanted to do
when they got back, after their big reception in the airport with
everyone waving bouquets and crying and pushing in to shake the
hands that had blessed and baptized new foreign Mormons, was
teach us younger guys about the world, its peoples and their many

customs, so we would know what was waiting for us when we went off on our own missions someday.

"A significant fact about Koreans," Timothy Breeden told us one night, "is that they see Americans as spoiled. They admire our institutions, sure—democracy and that—but basically they think we're pretty soft."

We were sitting around in Timothy's bedroom, four of us boys who had come there straight from church, sipping hot cider his mother had made and handing around a stack of snapshots showing crowded streets and blurry statues. When one of us would linger with a picture or hold it up to the light to see it better, Timothy would sway out forward from where he sat cross-legged on his bed and give us an expert description.

"That's a Buddha you have in your hand," Timothy told me. "Buddhas are their gods." He took back the picture and waved it around. "Who can guess how old this figure is?"

Someone dumb said, "A hundred years," like someone dumb always says.

Timothy looked at me. "Guess, Karl. Can you guess?"

I shook my head and tried not to yawn. I had run out of comments for Timothy. I had been in his room for over two hours, curious at first, then bored, waiting along with the other boys for Timothy to tire himself out. He had been back in Phoenix only three days and I could see he needed rest—there were shadows under his eyes and in his cheeks—but when I had asked him a moment ago if we should leave so he could go to bed, he'd told me he didn't need to sleep now that he knew how to meditate. "I don't have to eat as much, either," he said. "You can go a whole day on one slice of bread—you just have to burn it slowly."

"But don't you need liquids, too?" asked Kevin Smith. Kevin's cousin Donna was the girl who'd been picked by Bishop Geertz to write Timothy letters in Korea. At church that day, when Donna heard that Timothy was inviting us over, she had asked me to call her afterwards and give her a report.

"In point of fact," said Timothy, turning over his hands in his lap and staring at his palms, "liquids are *all* you need."

I looked at Kevin, whose eyes had gone wide, and wondered what I was going to tell Donna.

Probably that she would just have to wait.

D O N N A S M I T H was seventeen, six months older than me, and a popular girl in our school because of her nonstop activities schedule. She captained the volleyball "A" squad, she starred in the aqua-ballet, and whenever there was a charity drive to help the school buy new computers or combat muscular dystrophy worldwide, Donna would chair the planning committee and be the person who painted fresh red lines on the funds barometer next to the flagpole. The reason she had time for all these things was that she never studied. Beautiful Mormon girls don't have to. Chances are they'll be married by eighteen, or, if they want to go to college, BYU or Ricks will accept them no matter how low they graduate.

To keep the non-Mormon boys from bothering Donna while she was writing to Timothy, I had pretended to be her boyfriend. We even went out on dates together. Her rule was that I could touch her in public but not when we were alone. I obeyed. I liked Donna plenty—any boy would have who'd seen her perform, exploding out of water, *ta da!*—but what was I supposed to do? Donna had made it clear to me that keeping her faithful to Timothy was a duty I had to take seriously, or lose.

"You watch, he's going to appreciate this," Donna would often tell me, usually at the end of a date when we were sitting around in my Nova, digging the popcorn hulls out of our molars and trying to say good-bye without kissing. "You'll want to feel secure too," she'd tell me, "when you go away."

"I guess so," I'd say. "I suppose."

"Don't fool yourself," Donna would say. "You will. Out there all alone like that, having to cook your own meals. Not only that, they have riots there. Timothy says he got caught in one. Riots and murders all day long."

"You're right," I'd say. "It must be awful. I'll see you tomorrow. It's late."

"Well, don't just *agree* with me," Donna would say, giving my knee a backhanded slap that made her charm bracelet jingle. "Tell me what you *think*."

Sometimes, these talks would go on for so long and would get so incredibly pointless and dumb that I would have to climb out of the car and walk around the front and open Donna's door for her.

With Timothy home from Korea, though, Donna should have been through with me. According to the deal we'd made, I was supposed to watch from the sidelines as Donna and Timothy got engaged, went off to BYU together, and eventually set up house in one of the married dormitories there. That was Donna's plan, the plan that had worked so well for other couples, including her parents and my older sister. But Timothy had been home for three months and he still hadn't asked her out.

"Karl, can we talk?" Donna asked me at school one day. I took this as a kind of joke. I laughed. We were sitting in the library, where talking was all we ever did.

You had to have a book open though, so I balled up my sheet of doodles and opened one of Donna's books: *Crime and Punishment.*

"What are you reading this for?" I said. It made me sad that a girl with her looks suddenly felt she had something to gain by reading classic foreign literature.

Donna said, "Timothy's so confused now. Did you hear that he got an apartment downtown? His parents tried to stop him, so he borrowed a hundred dollars off Kevin to make the security payment."

All I said was, "Huh." Except for the downtown part, this sounded to me like good news. Timothy was twenty-one years old, he spoke a foreign language now—a tough one. He couldn't very well stay in that bedroom with Disneyland curtains and Noah's Ark wallpaper.

"I heard that he doesn't have furniture," she said. "No sofa, no table, no lamp." Donna looked at me, pausing, as if she thought I needed time to picture an empty room. "I want you to visit him, Karl. There's something I want you to give him for me."

"All we can give him," I said, "is love and patience." It was a thing I could say without thinking that sounded like something I'd thought about.

Donna didn't seem to hear me. She lifted her knapsack off the chair back and took out a fat brown envelope crisscrossed with black electrical tape.

"Can't you just mail this?" I said.

"No," said Donna. "They open things."

I reached across and touched the envelope. I knew I would probably open it myself, so I thought it was only right to give her a second chance: "Have Kevin take it."

Donna shook her head. "Kevin's a Buddhist now too, Karl. Someone stable has to do this, someone who's on *my* side."

Then Donna leaned over and kissed me on the cheek.

We were in public, so it was allowed.

THERE HAD BEEN cases worse than Timothy's—of boys who came home from the mission field actually physically wounded, or on drugs, or in love with a girl from wherever they'd taught, or even in love with the boy they'd taught with, since Mormons go off on their missions in pairs. The same way I knew what went on in the Temple without ever having been inside the Temple—mostly from overhearing my parents or talking with friends who had overheard theirs—I knew about boys who lost weight in the field and never gained it back, a worm in their stomachs that just dug in for life, and of one boy who went away to New Guinea and witnessed a levitation in the jungle, and could not forget it, and lived in his car now, thirty-four years old.

I was thinking all this as I drove down Central, a straight shot south between palm trees and malls to Timothy's new apartment. I had Donna's envelope up on the dashboard, with all the tape stuck back in place, and I was driving slowly, buying time, because of what I was delivering.

The pictures must have been taken with a timer—Donna propping the camera on a shelf, then scurrying backwards into position, with only seconds to fluff up her bangs and settle her hands on the hips of her swimsuit. Some of Donna's poses I recognized from spectacular moments in the aqua-ballet. Other poses she must have seen in fashion magazines. One shot showed her suit strap slipping off, accidentally on purpose, it looked like. No matter what the pose was, though—whether Donna's arms were up or down, doing an arching backwards dive or softly paddling out toward the camera—her mouth was always stern, a line, as if she did not plan to do this again and wanted that fact known.

Not by me, of course, but by Timothy. He was the one she was trying to save, and I had no choice but to help her.

THE LOW ADOBE apartment building was set around a gravel courtyard junked up with lawn chairs and tipped-over trikes and ruled by a pack of runty Mexicans playing

138

whatever game those kids play instead of Cowboys and Indians. The kids carried pistols and droopy plastic swords. The moment I closed the gate behind me, two little girls with lopsided crew cuts charged at my knees and held on tight as three screaming boys closed in with machetes. Stripping the girl's small hands off my legs, I remembered something my dad had told me: that if the Apostles sent me to Mexico, I should try to get out of it by pretending I couldn't learn Spanish, because there is just no helping those people.

Some of the doors I passed had number stickers, but most of them just had number-shaped stains where the stickers had rotted away in the sun. I slipped the envelope under my waistband, thinking it would be safer there, and flopped out my shirt to hide it.

When I finally found the right-numbered door, Kevin, not Timothy, answered my knock. He was barefoot, with only gym shorts on, and over his shoulder I could see furniture—not a whole lot, but enough.

"Karl, my man," said Kevin, waving me in with two splinted fingers wrapped in dirty tape.

I sat on the couch. "Where's Timothy?" I said.

Kevin said, "Supply run. He'll be back."

"What happened to your hand?" I said.

"See that cinder-block wall?" said Kevin. I looked. "Someday I'm going to master it," he said. "Someday I'll be stronger than that wall."

I wasn't really listening. I was searching the room for signs of Buddhism and not finding any. I did see a Book of Mormon, though: it was on the floor by my feet, weighted by a filthy clamshell ashtray. I leaned down to take the ashtray away and I felt Donna's envelope bending, all those pictures.

"Leave that ashtray be," said Kevin. "Everything has a place in this apartment."

I straightened back up, embarrassed. "Is Timothy teaching you something?" I said.

Kevin shrugged. "Stuff about Korea, that's all."

"Stuff like what?" I said.

"Tae-Kwon-Do karate, different techniques to focus my mind. Mostly, we just smoke here, though. That's why Timothy took this place, to have a place to smoke."

"Just to smoke?" I said.

Kevin nodded. "Timothy picked it up in Korea. He says he can't quit—he's a smoker now. He's breaking the Word of Wisdom and he doesn't know what to do. He'll probably leave the church about it."

"Smoking?" I said. "That's all that's going on here?"

"Pretty much," said Kevin. "What's sad is that Timothy knows he'd be perfect if this one thing wasn't ruining him."

I thought about this for a while. Then I said, "That's crazy. He should just ask the bishop for help. Bishop Geertz was a smoker once himself."

"You don't understand," said Kevin. "Timothy's not at that stage anymore. He doesn't ask for help. He stands alone."

"Does that go for Donna, too?" I said. "I hope he knows she's crying every night."

Just for a moment, Kevin looked angry—I watched his jaw muscles bunch together—but then, and it was amazing how he did this, he looked to the side and shut his eyes and when he turned back to look at me again his face was like a baby's, all washed-out and bright.

"That's none of my business," said Kevin. "Not yours, either."

Nothing else was said until I asked if I could use the bathroom. I wanted to adjust the envelope, and maybe have one last look at the pictures, especially that falling-strap one.

"Sorry, the toilet's dry," said Kevin. "We hardly ever use it."

He picked at his splint and eyed the wall. "We're at this stage where we hardly ever have to."

I told him that sounded very unhealthy.

"Only to Westerners," Kevin said.

A LOAF OF BREAD, a jug of grape juice, a carton of filterless Camels—that's what came out of Timothy's bag when he finally got back from the store. He set out his items neatly on the shelf, lining them up so they didn't touch, as if he planned to do a painting of them. I noticed then that his furniture was also spaced for a painting.

"You here for a karate lesson?" Timothy asked me. "Or just as a spy for the brotherhood?" A cigarette was burning in his fingers, but I hadn't seen him puff on it yet.

"I wanted to see how you're doing," I said. I felt the envelope poking my rib cage. "I wasn't in church last week."

"Nor, alas, was I," said Timothy, using a word I'd read in books but had never actually heard in life. He tapped off his ash on the leg of his jeans and rubbed it in with the heel of his hand. "I presume you have scoped why that is," he said.

It struck me then that Timothy had forgotten how to speak English in Korea and was building a whole new language for himself.

Kevin, starting to pace and chop the air, said, "Come on, let's go outside. We'll get all the kids and hold a class for Karl."

Timothy dragged on his cigarette. "You go ahead, Number Two. I'll be out in a triple jiff."

When Kevin had gone outside, Timothy stubbed out his cigarette, then lit a second one and frowned at me. At the edge of his still short haircut, just above and in back of his ear, I noticed a white shaved circle divided in half by a line of fuzz. It looked like something someone had stamped there without his necessarily knowing it.

"More propaganda from Bishop Geertz," said Timothy. He pointed at my bulging shirt.

"It's from Donna," I said, bringing out the envelope. "It's personal, though, so you might want to—"

Timothy took the envelope from me and started peeling the tape off. His expression and all the smoke around his body made him look like a man in his own private vampire movie.

"She told me it's very personal," I said.

Timothy frowned and went on peeling. "Don't worry, I've seen these before," he said. "Or others of similar character."

Timothy held up the envelope and shook out the pictures onto the couch. Some of the worst ones landed faceup and Timothy lined them up on the cushion, making their corners even. He gazed at them for a moment, then picked out a butt from the ashtray on his knee, put it in his lips, and relit it. He squinted at the pictures through the smoke. "Which are your favorites?" he asked me.

I reached around to adjust my collar.

Timothy said, "The bending-over ones?"

I kept my mouth shut.

"Those are the saddest of all," he said. "She's pushing it in those. The essence of beauty is stillness and simplicity."

Kevin poked his head in the door then. "Any time," he said. "They're ready."

I glanced out into the courtyard. About a dozen barefoot Mexicans were standing in a perfect line, not moving.

"Warm them up," said Timothy. He looked at me, grinning. "My troops," he said. "Assuming the meek shall inherit the earth—and there is every evidence they will—what you want to be, Karl, if you're smart, you want to be a general of the meek."

That's when I pushed myself up off the cushion. "Donna told

me to tell you to call her. I see that you don't have a phone, though, so forget it."

"Hey, amigo. Chill," said Timothy. He shuffled the pictures into a pile and slid them back into the envelope. "For the pornography file," he said.

"Do whatever you want," I said.

Timothy shook his head. "At least she's learned some modesty," he said. "In Korea, she sent me the wide-open spaces. You know what I mean by the 'wide-open spaces'? Photograph-wise? Anatomy-wise? Ever seen a Korean girl open a bottle of Coke? No hands?"

I didn't know what to say to this. I didn't know how to breathe and still be here. Out in the courtyard, the kids were screaming now, shooting out their little fists and screaming.

What I said next was a line from TV, but I knew it was the only line there is. "She's not going to wait any longer," I said. "I'll make sure of that."

Timothy said, "You do that," and stood up off the couch. He held out the envelope stuffed with secret pictures. "I guess these are yours then," he said. "Sorry you can't have the others—I burned them."

I let him hand me the envelope.

"I want you to promise me something," said Timothy, standing in the doorway and kicking off his shoes. "Promise you'll go on a mission, Karl. I recommend it oh so highly. It helps you get your priorities straight when you see how outnumbered we are."

I REMEMBER THOSE next few days as a dangerous time when I couldn't stop laughing. Everything was a joke, except for jokes. Jokes seemed very serious to me. Other things, though—the sacrament service, the way it was only torn-up Wonder Bread, yet everyone kept it for ages on their tongue—

the president's hair on the morning news being whipped down flat by helicopter wind—even the thought of my sister's husband supposed to be some all-star saint because he'd converted a whole Brasilian village—all that kind of stuff just cracked me up no end.

If my parents had been at home I probably wouldn't have gone so crazy, but they were over in Mesa that week, staying with my sister and doing Temple work. They were baptizing the dead. They were standing knee-deep in a golden font and watching a TV screen flash the names of people who had died in ignorance, before Joseph Smith restored the Church and after Jesus started it. The Church had collected these names from books and grave-yards all over the world and had put them onto microfilm and stored them in a bomb-proof vault inside a Utah mountain. Every time another corpse's name flashed, Mom or Dad got dunked in its behalf.

Baptizing the dead—another laugh.

I did not go to school, my mood was that tricky. I was afraid I'd see Donna, and bite her—I didn't know what I might do. I stapled her pictures onto a string the way you show off Christmas cards and hung them over the tub in my bathroom. I liked to slide down under the water, watching the pictures blur away. I did this every night. Then, on my third day home, a friend stopped over and told me that Donna was home from school herself, exhausted after a marathon car wash held to raise money for vanishing sea turtles.

"Is Donna there?" I asked her father. I was standing in the living room, the phone cord spooled around my chest because I was slowly spinning in place, trying to calm myself down. The turning and turning living room walls with all their framed verses and family portraits felt like the cyclorama I'd seen once of Brigham Young crossing the plains, that same dizziness.

"Timothy's sent a note," said Donna before I could get a word in. "Listen, everyone's bawling here. Come get me."

HEADING OUT OF TOWN that evening, before we realized where we were driving, I tried to ask about Timothy's note, but Donna did not want to talk about that. "More sad confusion" was all she would tell me, and something about him moving to the mountains. She wanted to talk about science instead. It was high time she knew more about it, she told me, draping her arm around my neck, and as I drained my gas tank making what felt like pointless right turns, she asked me all kinds of heartbreaking questions she could have had answered in seventh grade, if only she'd paid attention then. Why do planets rotate? How can ships built of steel float in water? Why does a car need four different gears?

When I told her my answers would take some time, she said that she knew that but had to start somewhere, which made me wonder where Donna had been or where she would have ended up, not even knowing the sun was a star.

And then we saw the sign and knew we had been driving somewhere after all.

Check-in was easy. The key fit the lock. The curtains were already drawn. The hardest part of our first time together there in the Day Rates Motel was pretending we didn't know what we were doing. It was having to fake we were virgins, though we were.

A Note About the Author

Walter Kirn lived on a farm in Minnesota up until
the time he went off to undertake his schooling. He
was graduated from Princeton summa cum laude,
and thereafter took a master's degree at Oxford
University. Mr. Kirn is married and lives in New
York City.

A Note on the Type

The text of this book was set in Sabon, a type face designed by Jan Tschichold (1902–1974), the well-known German typographer. Because it was designed in Frankfurt, Sabon was named for the famous Frankfurt type founder Jacques Sabon, who died in 1580 while manager of the Egenolff foundry.

Based loosely on the original designs of Claude Garamond (c. 1480–1561), Sabon is unique in that it was explicitly designed for hot-metal composition on both the Monotype and Linotype machines as well as for film composition.

Composed by The Sarabande Press,
New York, New York.
Printed and bound by Fairfield Graphics,
Fairfield, Pennsylvania.
Designed by Anthea Lingeman